PAUL STEWART

THE MIDNIGHT HAND

CORGI YEARLING BOOKS

THE MIDNIGHT HAND
A CORGI YEARLING BOOK : 0 440 863481

First published in Great Britain by Corgi Yearling Books

PRINTING HISTORY
Corgi Yearling edition published 1997

5 7 9 10 8 6 4

Set in 12/14.5pt Linotype New Century Schoolbook by
Phoenix Typesetting, Ilkley, West Yorkshire

Corgi Yearling Books are published by
Random House Children's Books,
61–63 Uxbridge Road, Ealing, London W5 5SA,
in Australia by Transworld Publishers,
c/o Random House Australia Pty Ltd,
20 Alfred Street, Milsons Point, NSW 2061,
and in New Zealand by Transworld Publishers,
c/o Random House New Zealand,
18 Poland Road, Glenfield, Auckland.

Made and printed in Great Britain by
Cox & Wyman Ltd, Reading, Berkshire

For Julie, Joseph and Anna

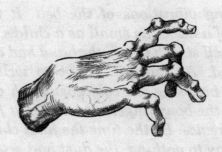

PROLOGUE

Black clouds swept across the moon as the bell at Styles Grange School began to toll. It was midnight, and there was mischief in the air.

High up in the bell-tower, that first deafening clang had sent the roosting pigeons flapping nervously this way and that in the dusty chamber. Time and again they collided with one another, before spilling out through the arched window openings and into the dark night. Now – as the bell continued to ring – the birds were flying round and round the tower, waiting for the din to subside.

It wasn't only the pigeons whose rest had been so rudely disturbed by the insistent chiming. In a dark and narrow recess, something else had felt

7

the echoing vibrations of the bell. It was the skeleton of a hand, as small as a child's.

As the bell struck seven, the hand had twitched and flexed. At nine, it began to writhe and squirm – breaking the cobwebs which clung so tightly to the bony fingers. At eleven it fell back into the crevice. By the time the final chime had faded away to nothing, the dust had settled and the hand was motionless once more.

Now the bell was silent, the pigeons returned to the tower. They swooped in and landed, all together, in a flurry of wings. Immediately, the air was filled with the sound of impatient cooing, as the birds strutted to and fro, jostling with one another for a good position. But the noise did not last for long. One by one, the pigeons settled down, plumped up their feathers and put their heads back under their wings. Within seconds, they were all asleep.

The hand, however, was not. Although you could hardly describe it as being awake, there was no doubt that it was once again aware.

It knew where it was. It recognized the touch of the dry crumbling mortar under its bony fingers.

It knew what it was: a hand that would find no lasting peace until it was once again reunited with the rest of the body. The inscription on the grave had seen to that.

Most importantly, the hand knew why it had been roused – at least in general terms. It was,

8

after all, the fourth time that its spirit had been roused. The details would, no doubt, be filled in later on.

Three times already it had failed to achieve what had to be done in the allotted time. Perhaps this time it would be luckier. Certainly it would try. The pain of separation had continued for too long.

And woe betide anyone who stood in its way.

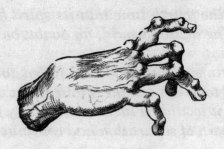

1

A BAD OMEN

'There it is!' cried Mrs Selkirk, as they rounded a particularly sharp corner. 'Look, Tom,' she said excitedly. 'We've made it! Welcome to your new school.'

Tom looked. Sure enough, about a hundred metres further on, there were the familiar gateposts. A solitary magpie was perched on the top of one of the wrought-iron gates. Tom's heart sank.

'And not before time, either,' Mr Selkirk said gruffly.

Tom said nothing. He knew his dad meant only that he was glad to be leaving the narrow lanes at last. He hadn't liked the sound of the leafless branches scraping along the sides of the car. 'There'll be hell to pay if it's scratching my paintwork,' he'd said more than once.

Tom's dad was extremely proud of his car. It was a sleek, white Mercedes. He'd bought it new, thirty-three years earlier, and it didn't have a mark on it.

Yes, Tom knew that it was concern for his car that made his dad come out with the *not-before-time* comment. All the same, it was a tactless remark. It made it sound as if he couldn't wait to see the back of his son. And his mum's enthusiasm didn't help either.

Tom sighed miserably and sat back in his seat. *He* would have been happy if the journey to school could have lasted for ever.

He watched the sign flash by; gold letters on varnished wood. STYLES GRANGE BOARDING SCHOOL, it announced. Tom felt a lump in his throat. The moment he had been dreading for so long had finally arrived. For the second time in his life, he was to be sent away.

It was the fourth of January; Tom wouldn't see his parents again until Easter – and he would miss them. Even though his mum could be loud and excitable, even though his father was tactless, Tom would miss them both, very much.

He was just about to tell them as much when Mr Selkirk suddenly slammed on the brakes, pushed the gear-stick into reverse and backed up. The magpie let out a raucous screech and flapped off over the playing fields. Mr Selkirk stopped next to the sign and turned to his wife.

'I thought the principal's name was Buchanan,' he said.

'It is,' said Tom's mum. 'Doctor Phillip Darcy Buchanan. Don't you remember? Ph.D Buchanan, Ph.D. We laughed about it . . .'

Mr Selkirk nodded impatiently. 'Then who is *that*?' he said, and pointed. All three of them stared at the words in the bottom right-hand corner of the board. Freshly painted gold letters announced that the principal was now one A.W.L. Bennett.

It was back in the middle of September that Tom and his parents had first come to look over the school. At the time, all three of them had liked the headteacher. Dr Buchanan was a tall, portly man with thick white hair and a bright red face. He had impressed Mr and Mrs Selkirk with the school's academic record, and won Tom over with his talk of the swimming pool and gym – and the football team which had finished second in the local league earlier that year.

'I'm sure you'll be very happy here,' he'd said to Tom.

'I'm sure he will,' Mr Selkirk had answered for him.

Tom, of course, had been less than sure – and yet, as the time approached, it was the thought of Dr Buchanan that had kept him going. Any school run by such a friendly old man couldn't be all bad. Now, it seemed, he was gone. Tom wondered nervously what this A.W.L. Bennett would be like.

'I don't mind if you change your mind,' he said hopefully. 'I mean, you don't know anything about this new head . . .'

'Nonsense,' his dad interrupted cheerfully. 'Styles Grange is an excellent school. If Dr Buchanan has gone, I'm sure they'll have picked an excellent replacement. Let's go and see what he's like.'

With that, Mr Selkirk eased the gears into first and set off again. The car jangled and jolted its way over the cattle grid and on up the steep drive. As they came over the brow of the hill, Styles Grange loomed into view. Tom gasped. It wasn't only the headteacher who had changed. The school itself was nothing like the place he remembered.

On that bright, sunny afternoon in September, the building had looked warm and inviting. Built from the local pinky-grey stones, it was nestling cosily in among the orange beech trees and crimson maples. This was the scene that had been chosen for the school prospectus. Now, however, the leaves were gone. Silhouetted against the curdled, grey sky, Styles Grange looked gaunt and grim and imposing.

As he stared ahead in horror, Tom realized he

was trembling. If they'd advertised the school with a photo of how it looked now, he would never have agreed to come. With its towers and turrets and spiral chimney stacks, Styles Grange School was straight out of Tom's spookiest nightmares.

Far ahead of him, the magpie reappeared and circled the building, once, twice, three times. Tom shivered with foreboding. Something bad was going to happen there; he just knew it!

2

MISS!

Tom's dad stopped the car at the top of the drive. The three of them climbed out and looked around. The courtyard was silent – in fact, the whole school seemed deserted.

Mr Selkirk tutted irritably and took the opportunity to inspect the paintwork on his car. Tom and his mum climbed the staircase which led up to the front entrance. At the top, Mrs Selkirk reached up and tugged the bell-pull. A clattering jangle echoed all round the hall inside.

Tom shuddered, and braced himself for the appearance of the one-eyed hunchback, or bandy-legged dwarf, or razor-toothed vampire – or whatever other monster might be lurking behind the heavy oak door with its black studs and curling hinges.

'I don't understand,' said Mrs Selkirk, and pulled at the rope a second time. Once again, the noise echoed round the cavernous hall.

'Perhaps we should come back when term starts,' said Tom.

'But we had a letter,' said his mum. 'Confirmation. They must be expecting us. Anyway, it has to be today – you know that.' She seized the bell-pull again.

At that moment, the door flew open, and Tom found himself staring at a short business-like woman dressed in a tartan skirt and jacket, with a nurse's upside-down watch pinned to her lapel. Although she was neither the hunch-back, dwarf nor vampire of his imagination, Tom felt anything but relieved. There was something about the way her pale blue eyes flicked back and forth between him and his mother which unnerved him.

'Yes?' she said.

'My name's Mrs Selkirk and this is . . .' his mum began.

The woman cut her short. 'I'm on the phone,' she explained. 'Come in and wait. I'll see to you as soon as I can.' And with that she was gone.

As he followed his mum into the hallway, Tom realized that even this had changed. Before, it had been warm and filled with the low murmur of children's voices; vases of dahlias and chrysanthemums had brightened every corner with a splash of colour. Now, the heating was off and the dark wood shelves were bare – and when Tom's dad joined them, his footsteps echoed ominously round the chilly air.

'Car seems fine,' he said, as he put Tom's bags down. 'Have you seen Mr Bennett, yet?'

Mrs Selkirk shook her head. 'His secretary told us to wait. She . . .'

From the far end of the hall, they suddenly heard the woman in question. She was clearly not pleased. Her strident voice cut through the silence like a rusty knife.

'I should warn you, Mr Pringle,' she screeched, 'I am not a woman to be trifled with. When I say a million, I *mean* a million – and if you're not interested, then I know plenty who are. Thank you and goodbye!' The sound of the receiver being slammed down echoed round the school like a bullet shot.

Mr and Mrs Selkirk looked at one another. Tom could see that even *they* were having second thoughts about the school. The trouble was, he also knew that at this late stage there was nothing they could do about it. However weird Styles Grange School was, they had no option but to leave Tom there.

*   *   *

Mr Selkirk was a banker. Most of the time, he was based in England – but not always. When Tom was seven, his dad had been sent to New York for two years. Since they hadn't wanted to interrupt his schooling, Tom's parents had sent him to Mallowbury, a small preparatory school for day-children and boarders. Tom had hated every minute there.

Things had suddenly improved shortly after his ninth birthday. Tom had received a letter to say that his dad had been offered a post in London. The following three years had been the happiest time of Tom's life. He had gone to the local middle school, and rediscovered all the things he had missed so much – friends coming round for tea; pancake and Hallowe'en parties; opening his birthday presents with his mum and dad. Little things. Ordinary things. Things that he had never really appreciated before.

Suddenly, it had all come to an abrupt end. Tom had sensed that something was wrong when his mum called him down from his bedroom.

'We've got some good news,' she'd said, smiling brightly. Tom looked down at the floor. His idea of good news and theirs were seldom the same. 'Your dad's been promoted.'

'Well done,' said Tom suspiciously.

'The thing is . . .' his mum went on.

'I'm not going back to Mallowbury!' Tom

shouted. Tears filled his eyes, blurring the pattern on the rug.

'Of course not, darling,' his mum had said. 'The thing is,' she repeated, 'the new bank *is* rather a long way and . . .'

'*How* far?' said Tom, sullenly.

'It's in Singapore,' his dad replied. 'The bank needs someone to set up a Far Eastern Division, and I've got the experience . . .'

'Take me with you,' said Tom quietly – the ache in his throat was almost too much to bear. He lifted his head and looked at them, one after the other; his mum and his dad. He knew they wanted him to be brave. But why should he make things easy for them? They were abandoning him. Again! 'Just take me with you,' he said, his voice cracked and close to sobbing. 'Please don't leave me.'

Of course, Mr and Mrs Selkirk were sympathetic. They hugged him. They kissed him. Both of them told him how much they loved him – after all, *that* was why they were sending him to boarding school. They would be bad parents if they let his education suffer. And didn't he think that *they* would miss *him*? Naturally, they would. But they would see each other in the holidays – the *long* holidays, that is; half-term breaks would be more difficult. Not that that would be a problem. The school they'd chosen was not only renowned both for its academic and

19

sporting achievements, but it was also very flexible. Tom would be able to start the week before the beginning of the Spring Term.

Tom's mum had shown him the school prospectus; the one with the building nestling in its autumn setting. 'Absolutely lovely,' she said.

'The best that money can buy,' his father had added.

And as Tom heard those words, he realized that he could never win the argument. They would never understand that what *he* wanted simply could not be bought.

'Doctor Buchanan assured us . . .' he heard his mum saying.

'But Dr Buchanan doesn't seem to be here now, does he?' his dad replied curtly. He checked his watch for the third time in as many minutes.

Tom smiled to himself. He knew the delay was upsetting his dad's tight schedule. 'Why don't we have a look round the grounds while we're waiting?' he asked innocently.

Tom's dad merely scowled and looked at the time again. 'Where *is* he?' he said angrily.

'Where is who?' came a voice from the far end of the corridor.

Mr Selkirk spun round. 'I, er . . . Mr Bennett,' he said.

'There is no Mr Bennett,' the woman replied,

20

as she clip-clopped across the hallway towards them.

Mr Selkirk looked perplexed. 'Mr *Bennett*,' he said. 'The principal. A.W.L. Bennett. I saw it quite clearly on the board at . . .'

The woman breathed in sharply. 'Agnes Winifred Letitia,' she said. 'Not all principals are men, Mr Selkirk.'

'No . . . I . . .' Tom had never seen his dad so flustered before. He watched him hold out his hand. 'James Selkirk,' he said. 'How do you do, Mrs Bennett?'

'*Miss* Bennett,' the woman said icily and, leaving Mr Selkirk's hand hanging in mid-air, she turned to his wife. 'Term does not commence until the eleventh,' she said. 'Today is the fourth.'

'I know . . . but . . . I have a letter,' she said, and rummaged in her handbag. 'From your . . . your predecessor,' she added.

Miss Bennett read the letter in silence. It was impossible to know what she was thinking. When she finally looked up and spoke, however, her words had lost their cutting edge.

'Dr Buchanan died tragically in November. A stroke,' she added in a reverent whisper. 'I was appointed in December. The transition has been largely smooth, but sometimes hiccups do occur. The school will, of course, honour its commitments – and I should apologize for its being so cold. We've had some problems with the boiler. It ought to be back in action tomorrow.' She turned to Tom and fixed him with those pale yet piercing blue eyes. 'Welcome to Styles Grange,' she said, and offered him her hand to shake.

For a second, Tom hesitated. After all, she had ignored his dad's hand. Then again, he didn't want things to get off to a bad start. As he reached out, Miss Bennett seized his hand and squeezed tightly.

Her hand was hard and bony, and as she pumped his arm up and down, Tom felt icy shivers coursing through his veins. He smiled weakly, and looked down.

At that moment, the door behind them swung open. A tall boy with short, dark hair walked in, noticed the people standing in the hall, and stopped.

'Ah, Asa,' said Miss Bennett. She turned to Tom's mum. 'Asa Martin,' she explained. 'He's also back a little early this term. You returned yesterday, didn't you, Asa?' she said. The boy nodded. 'Asa, we have a new boy here,' she went on. 'Since you will both be in the same dorm, I'd like you to go through the main school rules with him; show him the ropes. Can I trust you to do that?'

Asa nodded. 'Yes, miss,' he said.

Satisfied that the school – and its new principal – were all right after all, Mr and Mrs

Selkirk announced, in unison, that it was time they were off. Tom nodded. It was pointless trying to prolong their departure. He kissed his mum and, as he did so, she slipped a small present into his hand. 'From us both,' she whispered. Then he shook his dad's hand; Mr Selkirk did not approve of public shows of emotion.

'See you at . . . at Easter, then,' said Tom.

'The time will whizz by,' his mum said. 'You'll see.'

Tom smiled, picked up his bags and followed Asa across the hall and up the stairs. When he reached the top of the first flight, he stopped and looked back. His parents were already gone. Tom turned to the boy and smiled, embarrassed. 'Plane to catch,' he explained.

Asa nodded. 'There's two sorts of kids at Styles Grange,' he said. 'Half of them glad to come here to escape their parents, and the other half are sad that their parents want to escape them! The *glads* and the *sads*, that's what I call them.'

'What am I, then?' asked Tom.

'A *sad*,' said Asa. 'No doubt about it. Come on, let's dump your bags up in the dorm. It's nearly dinnertime. Afterwards, I'll show you all round the haunted house.'

The word echoed round Tom's head. Haunted! He'd *known* there was something spooky about the place, right from the start. But then again, he thought, Asa was probably just teasing – trying to see how gullible he was. The last thing he wanted to do was admit to being scared of things-that-go-bump-in-the-night: he'd never hear the end of it. He turned to Asa.

'Haunted house, eh?' he said, and smiled knowingly.

Instead of laughing it off, as Tom had thought he would, Asa shook his head. Tom felt apprehensive.

'You don't mean . . .'

'You'll see,' Asa said grimly. 'You'll see.'

3

IN THE DARK

As things turned out that evening, Asa never did get round to showing Tom around the school building. An increasingly terrifying sequence of events saw to that.

The dormitory was directly under the roof, up on the fourth floor. Tom was out of breath by the time he got there. The ceiling was low, beamed, and sloped down on one side of the room. Along the walls were two rows of six wooden beds, each with a small heart carved into the headboard. To the right of each one was a chest of drawers; to the left, a small bedside cabinet. The bare floorboards had been stripped and varnished. As well as a length of carpet that ran down the centre of the room, every bed had its own small rug.

Asa walked over to the windows – two small, leaded squares that looked on to the roof – and glanced out. 'You can pick any bed you like,' he said. 'Except that one,' he added, pointing to the bed behind him. 'That's mine.'

Tom walked up and down the strip of carpet, looking at each bed in turn. He didn't want to be in the middle of the room, but he liked the idea of sleeping on the side with the sloping ceiling. Being near a window sounded nice, too.

'I'll have this one,' he said finally, and plonked his bags down on the bed opposite Asa's. As he did so, he realized he was still holding the present his mum had given him. Asa saw it too.

'What's that?' he said, and came over to look.

'I'd forgotten all about it,' said Tom. With eager fingers, he peeled back the sticky tape and peeked inside the wrapping paper. Something red and shiny gleamed. He turned the whole lot upside down, and let the object drop into his hand.

Tom grinned. It was a Swiss Army knife – the Swiss Army knife he had been so disappointed not to get at Christmas. As well as the usual two blades, bottle opener, screwdrivers, corkscrew, tweezers, magnifying glass and the thick needle things he'd never worked out a use for, it also had a double-edged saw.

The moment he'd first seen the knife in the shop window, Tom had wanted it – not because he had some wood that desperately needed cutting, but because of the label which was tied to it. *Not recommended for persons under twelve years of age*, it said. Well, Tom was twelve now: twelve and a quarter, in fact. He was no longer a silly child who couldn't be trusted with a penknife. At the time, his mother had refused to give in. Something, he realized, must have changed her mind. Perhaps it had occurred to her that if Tom was old enough to live without his parents, he was old enough to cope with a double-edged saw. Whatever, the Swiss Army knife was fantastic – it was only a shame that it had been a 'farewell' present.

'Let's have a look,' said Asa. Tom handed it over and watched as Asa pulled out the various blades one by one. He was clearly impressed. 'A double-edged saw,' he said, and ran his thumb cautiously over the serrated edge. 'Very nice.' He pushed all the blades back into place and returned the knife to Tom. 'Cool,' he said. 'But you'd better not let Miss Bennett catch you with it. She'll confiscate it.'

Suddenly, something made Tom shudder. He couldn't tell what it was. He knew only that the mention of Miss Bennett had brought back the feel of her hard, bony, ice-cold hand; that, and the sight of Asa running his thumb over the razor-sharp blade. Somehow, the two things came together in his head, as if one had been superimposed on the other – as if they were both linked.

'Are you OK?' he heard Asa saying.

'Yes . . . I . . .' he said, looking round giddily.

'Just don't let her see it,' Asa went on.

Tom nodded. 'I won't,' he said. 'Asa,' he said a moment later. 'You know you said . . . you called the building a haunted house . . .'

'Ye-es?'

'Well, is it?' Tom said. 'Haunted, I mean?'

Asa looked away. He swallowed. 'Something's going on,' he said finally. 'But I don't know what.'

Tom stared at him. Asa looked genuinely worried. Either he was a brilliant actor, or there really was something happening at Styles Grange which the boy didn't understand. 'What sort of something?' Tom asked nervously.

'I'm not saying any more,' said Asa. 'If you *do* see anything, we can compare notes after.'

Tom fell silent. Asa's reluctance to talk was making him feel uneasy. Suddenly, the sound of the gong echoed up from the hallway.

'Dinner!' Asa announced, obviously glad that the subject had changed. 'Come on, I'm famished. Aren't you?'

'I was,' said Tom. 'But I seem to have lost my appetite.'

Asa turned and looked at him seriously. Tom stared back, wondering what he was going to tell him now. That the building was not only haunted, but also cursed perhaps; or that the dormitory had rats – Tom *hated* rats. He watched Asa's mouth break into a grin.

'Mrs Baxter's a brilliant cook,' he said.

As it turned out, Asa was right. Mrs Baxter's meal was delicious, and the cold made him extra hungry. Tom had seconds of both the lasagne and the lemon meringue pie.

While they were eating, the two boys talked. They discovered they both liked music, and swimming, and football. In addition, Asa boxed. 'My dad taught me,' he explained. 'He wanted me to be able to look after myself.' Asa's dad, Tom discovered, was a builder who had made a million or two when house prices were going up. Not that the money had made him happy. Mr and Mrs Martin were in the middle of an extremely messy divorce.

'Which is why I'm a *glad*,' Asa snorted. 'It was rotten being at home with the pair of them – rowing, arguing, fighting the whole time . . .' He laughed. 'And they were even worse with each other!'

Tom smiled. He didn't understand how Asa could talk about his home-life so lightly – but he was pleased that he did. It put his own situation into perspective. *He* would be staying with both his mum and his dad in the Easter holidays. By that time Asa, on the other hand, would probably have to choose which of his parents to visit – or spend two weeks with each. It was a decision Tom would have hated to make.

'Any more for any more?' said Mrs Baxter, as she bustled into the dining hall with the steaming bowl of lemon meringue pie in her hand.

'Not for me,' said Tom politely. 'It was delicious.'

'Absolutely fan-tas-tic, Mrs B!' said Asa.

'Mrs Baxter, to you, you cheeky rascal,' she said sternly, but Tom could see she was pleased with the compliment.

Mrs Baxter was, he thought, *exactly* what a good cook should look like. All sort of round and roly-poly, with smiley eyes and rosy cheeks. Tom liked her at once.

Just then, the door at the end of the dining hall opened, and Miss Bennett walked in. She strode up to the table and stopped between Tom and Asa.

'You've finished, have you?' she said to Asa.

'Yes, Miss Bennett,' he said.

'In that case, you'll be able to send these for me,' she said, and handed him a small bundle of letters.

Asa jumped up. 'In the postbox?' he said.

'No, Asa,' she said. 'I want you to go out, catch yourself seven pigeons and tie the letters to their legs. Of course, in the postbox!'

Asa nodded. 'Can Tom come as well?' he said.

'All right,' said Miss Bennett. 'But don't dawdle. I want to lock up.'

Out of the corner of his eye, Tom noticed Mrs Baxter shuffling awkwardly. From the look on her face – all purse-lipped and impatient – he guessed that the cook didn't have a very high opinion of Miss Bennett. He smiled at her as he got up from his seat. 'That was *really* nice,' he said. 'Thanks.'

'Glad you enjoyed it,' Mrs Baxter said, suddenly all smiley-eyed again. 'It's Gooey Chocolate Pud tomorrow,' she added. 'With butterscotch sauce . . .'

'Yes, yes; all very interesting, I'm sure,' Miss Bennett interrupted. 'Tom, if you're going with Asa, would you please go now. The late collection is in . . .' she consulted her watch, 'eight minutes exactly.'

'Yes, Miss Bennett,' said Tom, as he hurried after his friend.

'And don't run in school!' she barked.

By the time Tom caught up with him, Asa was already halfway down the stairs. He was flipping through the envelopes, looking at the names and addresses.

'*Archer Antiques: Import/Export,*' he read out to Tom. '*Sully's Antiques and Curios. Grindlay and Swainson's Brass, Bronze and Copper Emporium. Antiques International.*

31

What do you think she's up to?'

Tom shrugged. 'How should I know?' he said. 'I've only been here three hours!'

'How about this one?' said Asa. *'Reginald Courteney Pringle, Esquire,'* he read out in his poshest voice. 'Sounds a right tonker . . .'

'Pringle?' said Tom. 'She was shouting at someone called Pringle earlier. On the phone. "When I say a million, I *mean* a million." That's what she said.' He glanced over at the envelope. It, too, was addressed to an antiques business. 'What's she actually like?' asked Tom.

'Miss Bennett?' said Asa. 'She's all right. Strict, but not unfair. Not as nice as Dr Buchanan, but . . . HEY!' he shouted, and pointed at the headlights which had stopped at the end of the drive. 'It's the post van. Come on!'

As the bell in the chapel tower mournfully chimed the hour, Asa and Tom raced headlong down the track. They arrived at the letter-box just as the postman was locking its door.

'Lucky you caught me, lads,' he said, as he took the letters and popped them into his sack. 'There's terrible storms forecast. They say trees might come down – and if they do, there's no knowing how long it'll take to clear the roads round here.'

Storms! thought Tom miserably, as he and Asa made their way back up the hill. 'Cut off!' he groaned. 'Here!' Just the thought of it was appalling.

He stared at the sinister building looming up in front of him. Harsh shadows cast by the almost-full moon made it look creepier than ever, and the lights inside did nothing to soften the air of grim foreboding.

At the bottom was the lamp, illuminating the porch with its yellow glow. It made the doorway look like a gaping mouth, toothless and angry – with the staircase below sticking out like an insolent tongue. High up in the roof above were two more lights. Although Tom knew they were only the windows in the dormitory, he shuddered. They were glinting like the eyes of some predatory beast.

Then, all at once, as if the animal had been blinded, the lights went out. All of them. In the dormitory, in the doorway, and all down the driveway; even the lamps on the gateposts stopped shining. And as black clouds rolled in from the west, blotting out the moon, Tom and Asa found themselves in complete darkness.

Tom was close to tears. Storms, being cut off – and now a power cut! 'I don't like it,' he murmured.

'Grab hold of my jacket,' said Asa. 'As long as we stick to the track we'll be OK.'

Tom did as he was told, happy that Asa seemed willing to take control. And yet, as the two boys made their way slowly uphill, Tom's heart began to pound furiously. What they were doing was wrong. They shouldn't be struggling to get back to the building. They should be running in the opposite direction, as fast as they could, to escape the growing evil that was at the heart of Styles Grange.

What they *should* do and what they *could* do were, however, two entirely different matters. Neither Tom nor Asa had anywhere else to go.

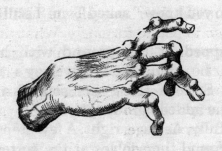

4

UNDER ATTACK

The darkness wrapped itself round the two boys like a monstrous, pitch-black blanket. They could no longer see the building ahead of them; they couldn't even see their hands in front of their faces. What was worse, the darkness was so complete, so impenetrable, that their eyes would never get used to it. Blindly they stumbled on, while all around them the sounds of the night filled the air. Owls hooted, rodents screeched; some distance to their left, a fox yelped. To Tom and Asa, it sounded like a wolf howling for the moon to return.

'Nearly there,' Asa said encouragingly. 'We're just coming into the car-park now.'

'How do you know?' asked Tom. 'I still can't see a thing.'

Asa tapped at the ground with his shoe. 'Tarmac,' he said. 'The driveway's made of concrete. Sort of thing the son of a builder notices,' he added, and laughed.

Thankfully, Asa was right. A few steps further on, they found themselves at the bottom of the stairs. Tom let go of Asa's jacket and made his way up. Despite himself, he was relieved to have escaped the awful nothingness outside. Here, at least, was something with shape and form – even if the staircase did lead up to Styles Grange itself.

The heavy door was on the latch. They pushed it, and went in.

'There you are!' came a voice. It was Mrs Baxter. She hurried towards them, with a blazing hurricane-lamp in each hand. 'I was just on my way down to find you,' she said.

'Bit early for lights-out, isn't it, Mrs B?' said Asa.

Mrs Baxter tutted impatiently. 'It's the generator,' she said. 'Miss Bennett's got my Clifford working on it now. As if he hasn't got enough on his plate, what with the boiler and the cool-room . . .'

'The cool-room?' said Asa.

'There's something wrong with the thermo-

36

whatsit,' she said. 'It won't get cold enough.' She looked round the dark hallway and snorted. 'It won't get cold at all now – *and* we've just had a big delivery in,' she went on. 'Still, far be it from me to say "I told you so"!'

She handed Asa one of the lamps. 'There,' she said. 'Till the power comes on.'

Asa immediately held it up like a lantern, and began singing *We Wish You a Merry Christmas*. His voice – which was on the verge of breaking – yodelled round the darkness overhead. He stopped abruptly, thrust out his hand towards Mrs Baxter. 'Spare us a couple coins, missus?' he said.

'Asa Martin!' she laughed. 'I do declare you are the cheekiest boy I have ever come across. Get away with you now – and be careful with that lamp,' she called out, as he and Tom started up the stairs.

Zig-zagging his way up the eight flights of stairs, Tom realized that his fear had returned. His scalp was prickling, his palms were clammy, and his heart was beating so hard it felt as if it were about to explode. Asa wasn't helping matters. He was swinging the lamp slowly to and fro; a motion which sent long, dark shadows darting this way and that. What was more, at the top of each flight of stairs, he would pause, peer round the corner and groan

37

spookily. 'Whoooooaaaeerr!'

By the third floor, Tom had had enough. 'Will you stop that?' he snapped.

Asa glared round at him. For a moment, Tom thought things were going to get nasty. The next second, however, Asa's expression softened. 'Sorry, mate,' he said. 'I didn't . . . Come on, let's go and get our wash stuff. I'll show you where the bathroom is.'

The boys' wash area was a long thin room at the far end of the corridor. Asa placed the lamp on a shelf next to a mirror, doubling its brightness. Since the hot water was still off, they both made do with a quick hand-and-face-wash. The icy water felt good on Tom's burning cheeks.

As he was brushing his teeth, he glanced at Asa's face in the mirror – and back to his own reflection. He realized how young he looked in comparison. Not only was Asa's voice breaking, but there was already hair growing above his top lip. He was taller than Tom, and much more powerfully built; the boxing had clearly had an effect on his twelve-year-old body.

The thing was, Tom also knew that Asa – big, strong Asa, who had been taught to look after himself – was as frightened as he was. He was just better at covering it up.

Something was out there, that much was certain; some unseen devilry lurking in the shadows of Styles Grange. It would take more than physical strength to destroy its terrible power once and for all. The two boys would have to be cunning, resourceful, determined; they would need nerves of steel and an iron will. They would also have to stick together.

Back in the dormitory, Tom unpacked his bags and put his clothes away in the drawers. With his alarm clock and a framed family photo on the cabinet, his books standing on top of the chest of drawers, and a poster of *the Raz* up on the sloping roof above his bed, his corner of the room was beginning to look a bit more homely.

It was only as he was stuffing his duffle bag in the hold-all, and putting both into his suitcase, that Tom noticed Mister Bear. Although he'd told her not to bother, his mum had packed him after all. Tom was pleased. The sight of his teddy's friendly face made him feel better than he had all day. Nevertheless, for the first time since the generator had broken down, Tom was glad that the lights weren't on. In the shadowy lamplight, he was able to slide the bear under his quilt without Asa seeing. Mister Bear did not like to be laughed at.

'Hey, Tom,' Asa said.

Tom spun round guiltily. 'Yes?' he said.

Asa nodded towards the hurricane-lamp. It was flickering ominously. 'You'd better get a move on,' he said. 'The light's about to give up.'

Tom shut his case and kicked it under the bed.

'I've finished now,' he said. As he spoke, the flame gave a final flash of bright light, sputtered, and went out. The dormitory was plunged into darkness – not, however, before Tom noticed something. Something which struck him as strange, yet reassuring.

It was still only eight o'clock, but with no light, there was nothing they could do. Tom and Asa climbed into their beds and wished each other a good night.

Tom lay on his back, hands behind his head, staring at the wall. The moon came out again. It shone milkily behind the thinning clouds. And as his eyes slowly grew accustomed to the darkness, Tom found he could make out the square outlines of the windows; dark grey against the black.

'Asa?' he said.

'Yes,' came the muffled reply.

'What was that I saw on your pillow?'

'On my . . .?' He heard Asa chuckle. 'That's Paddy the Panda,' he said.

'I thought it was a panda,' said Tom. He paused. 'Only . . .'

'Yes.'

'Well, aren't you . . .? Doesn't your dad ever say you're a bit old for cuddly toys?'

Asa laughed again. 'He's my mascot,' he explained. 'The only time I ever lost a fight was when I forgot to take Paddy along to the ring.

Paddy and I go back a long way.'

Tom fell silent. He saw again how different he and Asa were. True, they both had furry toys, but the difference remained. Mister Bear was a comforter; Paddy the Panda was a lucky mascot. Still, now he'd brought the subject up, Tom thought that he ought to continue.

'I've got a bear,' he confessed. 'Mister Bear. I've had him since I was a baby.'

'I know,' said Asa. 'I saw him. Night, Tom.'

Tom rolled happily over on to his side. He hugged Mister Bear tightly to his chest. 'N'night, Asa,' he said.

It was only when he woke up that Tom realized he'd been asleep. It was still night-time, and outside a raging wind was buffeting the windows and howling down the chimneys – not that it was the wind which had woken Tom. The chapel bell was tolling – its loud, echoing clang splintered the silence time and again. But it wasn't the bell which had woken him either.

All at once, Tom felt something cold and dry stroking his cheek. His blood ran cold. *That* was what had woken him!

He sat bolt upright in bed, and flailed wildly – blindly – with his arms. Something was there! Something had touched him – yet, no matter where he reached out to, his fingers felt nothing. He felt cold, hot, cold again; his mouth was dry.

'Where are you?' he whispered.

As if in response, he felt something tickling him under the chin.

'No!' he screamed. The tickling abruptly stopped.

Tom winced and stared around him, wild-eyed. For a moment, the dark clouds thinned, and the dormitory was once again bathed in soft moonlight.

Suddenly, out of the corner of his eye, Tom saw a movement. He spun round. Something – were they claws? – glinted in the moonlight. The next moment, in a blur of movement, the thing scampered under the bed. Tom sat there, too terrified to move. The darkness returned.

What could it have been? A giant cockroach? A lobster? Certainly it had *looked* like a lobster. But what on earth would a lobster be doing in the top dormitory of a school situated so far away from the sea?

The bell was still chiming as the room grew dark once more. Beneath him, Tom could hear the thing scuttling about on the bare boards beneath his bed. *Squeak, scratch, squeaky-scratch*. It was doing something. But what? Tom was far too frightened to look. He pulled his legs up and hugged them to his chest. Anyway, he thought, it's too dark to see anything.

Suddenly, the moon came out again – and this time in its full glory. It lit up the dormitory better than the hurricane-lamp had done. Now Tom had no excuse.

Slowly, cautiously, Tom leant over to the side of the bed. With one hand on the bed-frame and the other on the cabinet – ready for a quick getaway – he eased himself down. Past the mattress, past the quilt he went. The blood pounded in his ears as he got closer and closer to the floor. Finally, head upside down, he found himself staring in under the bed.

Despite the moonlight, it was still dark there. For a moment, Tom thought that the thing must have gone. And then he saw it!

It was crouching down in the shadows by the far bed-leg. Although it was still impossible to make out what it was, Tom could see it moving. It was twitching and flexing – like a cat about to pounce.

He should have taken this as a warning. As it was, Tom was too intent on trying to see what the thing actually was, and when it suddenly leapt at him, he was not quick enough to pull himself out of the way. He screwed his eyes shut, and winced as something cold and rubbery brushed roughly past his cheek. Instinctively, Tom raised his hand to his face – and promptly crashed to the floor.

He looked up to see the thing scuttling round the end of the bed and out of sight. Abruptly, the dormitory was plunged into darkness. And yet, against the dark grey window, Tom saw its silhouette – more a starfish than a lobster now – as it leapt against, and through, the glass.

Tom leapt to his feet and ran to the window. The glass wasn't broken. The thing had simply passed through as though there was nothing there.

He seized hold of the handle and tried to push the window open. In vain. Something was stopping it from moving. Tom rattled the window furiously. He had to see where the thing had gone. He just had to.

All at once, the whole dormitory blazed with light. Tom screamed. Asa jumped up, and stared around him in terror. 'What? What? What?' he cried out.

'It's . . . it's only me,' Tom stuttered. 'I . . . I'm sorry I screamed. The light made me jump.'

Asa rubbed his eyes. 'Power must be back on,' he said, and yawned. 'What were you doing out of bed?' he said.

'I . . . I thought I saw something,' said Tom.

Instantly wide awake, Asa looked at Tom sharply. '*What* did you see?'

Tom shrugged. 'I'm not sure,' he said. 'It sounds stupid but, well – it looked like a lobster.'

'A lobster,' said Asa. His face looked serious. 'I said we'd compare notes if you saw something, didn't I?' he muttered. He took a deep breath and, as Tom looked on, he pulled up his pyjama sleeves. Then, with his left hand clutching his right arm just above the wrist, he tensed the fingers and let the whole right hand scamper across the bed. Asa looked up. 'Did it look like that?' he asked.

Tom realized that he was trembling from head to toe. 'Y . . . y . . . yes,' he stammered. 'That was . . . was *exactly* what it looked like. A hand.'

Asa nodded. He looked at Tom. 'Worse than that,' he said. 'Didn't you notice the ragged skin.'

Tom swallowed. He *had* noticed it: he'd thought it was the lobster's frilled tail. 'Ragged skin?' he said.

'Ragged skin,' Asa repeated. 'It's not just a hand. It's a *severed* hand.'

5

A GHOSTLY REFRAIN

Despite Mrs Baxter's excellent fry-up, Asa and Tom were subdued over breakfast the following morning. Neither of them had slept well. Although the hand made no more reappearances that night, there were several times when they thought it had. The old building had creaked and groaned under the constant battering from the wind. And with each creak, and with each groan, Asa and Tom had snapped their eyes wide open, and stared round anxiously to see whether the ghoulish hand had returned.

'What do you think we should do, then?' asked Tom finally.

Asa sighed. 'Well, first of all, we've got our morning meeting in the Junior Common Room

46

with Miss Bennett at ten o'clock. She insists
that . . .'

'That wasn't what I meant,' said Tom.

'I know,' said Asa, grumpily. He shrugged.
'What *can* we do?'

'Well,' said Tom slowly. 'There's usually a
historical reason for somewhere being
haunted . . .'

'You what?' said Asa.

'I mean, when a place has got a ghost,' Tom
explained, 'it's because something horrible
happened there in the past.'

'Yeah, well, something horrible *did* happen,'
said Asa. 'That's obvious. Someone's hand got
chopped off.'

'Exactly,' said Tom. 'So what we've got to find
out is whose hand it was, and why it was
chopped off.'

'Great,' said Asa unenthusiastically. 'And how
do we do that?'

Tom shrugged. 'I thought we could start in the
library,' he said. 'See if there's a book on Styles
Grange. If there is, we might find something
useful . . .'

At first, Tom thought Asa was going to dismiss
the idea. His brow was creased up in a
thoughtful frown. Suddenly, however, his face
broke into a grin.

'There *is* a book!' he said excitedly. 'I
remember Dr Buchanan showing us it once last

47

year. Come on,' he said, jumping up from the table. 'Let's go and have a look.'

By the time Mrs Baxter came back into the dining hall, the boys were gone. She was disappointed to see that their plates were not quite empty.

The library was on the first floor of Styles Grange. It had been put in by the previous owner over a hundred years earlier. When the school had taken over the premises fifty years later, the library was the only room not to be altered. As a result, it looked – and felt – much older than the rest of the building.

Tom looked round at the oak tables and green-leather upholstered chairs; at the rows of school photographs which covered the far wall; at the shelves which went from floor to ceiling on the three remaining walls. He had never seen so many books. There were thousands of them – perhaps hundreds of thousands.

'Where on earth do we start?' he groaned.

Since the books were filed by library code-numbers, and the index cabinet which listed these numbers was locked, their task seemed hopeless. They spent over an hour scanning the shelves for any book that looked relevant. By ten o'clock, both Asa and Tom realized that they were not going to find what they were looking for.

Disappointed that his idea had been thwarted,

48

yet not wishing to give up, Tom suggested that they looked round the rest of the school anyway. 'Perhaps we'll find some vital clue,' he said optimistically.

Asa glanced out at the torrential rain pouring down outside and shrugged. 'Might as well,' he said, and added, 'after we've seen Miss Bennett.'

'Oh yes,' Tom sighed. 'I forgot.'

Thankfully, the morning meeting didn't take long. Miss Bennett seemed as keen as the boys themselves to keep it as brief as possible. Since the weather was bad, she gave permission for Asa to show Tom around the school, reminding him not to go anywhere that was out of bounds. She asked them to clear the school fields of any rubbish when the weather got better. She gave them a reading list of books they should read before the beginning of term, and dismissed them with a stern 'stay out of mischief'.

'Yes, Miss Bennett,' both boys replied, and were gone.

They started their tour up on the third storey of the building: the floor beneath the dormitories. It was here that the classrooms were situated. Tom looked in at the succession of rooms – each with their rows of desks, their blackboard, globe and wallcharts – and sighed. On the second floor were the language centre, complete with individual listening booths, and the science laboratories. Back on the first floor, apart from the library, there were a games room and two common rooms – one for the juniors and one for the seniors.

Returning to ground level it struck Tom that, although quite interesting, their look round hadn't got them any closer to solving the mystery of the severed hand. He knew that, at some stage, he would have to return to the library for another look.

As they walked past the kitchens, Asa glanced in. 'Morning, Mrs B!' he shouted cheerily.

Mrs Baxter turned and put her hands firmly on her hips. 'My fried bread not to your liking this morning, eh?' she said.

'I . . . erm . . . No, it was as tasty as ever,' said Asa. 'I've just got this . . . a bit of a stomach-ache.'

A look of concern came over Mrs Baxter's face. 'Would you like some milk of magnesia?' she said. 'I can get some.'

Asa shook his head. 'I'll be fine,' he assured her. 'Honest – and thanks,' he said, and as they continued along the corridor, he explained to Tom that he hadn't wanted to say anything which might lead to talk of the hand. 'There must be some reason why the hand is appearing to us,' he said. 'Anyway,' he added. 'No-one would believe us even if we did tell them.'

Tom nodded, but said nothing. He, too, had been wondering why the pair of them had been singled out for the peculiar haunting. He remembered the size of the hand. It had been little bigger than his own. Perhaps it's a child's hand, he thought. Perhaps that's why it's trying to communicate with children. Tom kept his ideas to himself. He wasn't sure whether Asa would appreciate being called a child.

As they passed Miss Bennett's office, the woman herself suddenly appeared behind them. She looked distracted.

'Ah, Asa, Tom,' she said. 'Tomorrow's Morning Meeting is cancelled. I have some urgent business to attend to. I'll see you, as normal, on Thursday. All right?' And before they had even time for the 'Yes, Miss Bennett', she had disappeared back into her office and shut the door.

Asa looked at Tom and raised his eyebrows. 'Strange,' he commented. 'It'll be the first one she's missed. Not that I'm complaining!'

They continued on down to the end of the corridor. There, they turned left along a glass-sided walkway which took them beyond the original building.

'All the sports things are in the annexe,' Asa told him. 'There's the main hall – for basketball, five-a-side footy, and that; two squash courts, the swimming pool . . .'

'Can we go swimming later?' Tom interrupted.

Asa shook his head. 'I've tried it,' he said. 'It's absolutely freezing. We'll have to wait until the boiler's been fixed.' He continued walking. 'And last but not . . .' He stopped and frowned. 'Last but not least . . .' He turned to Tom. 'Can you *hear* something?' he whispered.

Tom listened. There *was* something: a sort of scratching, squeaking sound. A familiar sound. It was coming from the end of the corridor.

'That's w . . . what I heard last night,' he said, and shivered. 'W . . . what's down there?' he asked nervously.

'A small gym,' said Asa. 'For weight-training, you know.'

Tom nodded. He was trying to remain calm, but his imagination was busy working overtime. What if, sometime in the past, there had been some horrible accident on one of the machines – an accident which had led to someone's hand being severed? What if the hand was there now, waiting to pounce on them as they walked in? He swallowed nervously. 'Maybe we should come back another time,' he said.

'Rubbish,' said Asa, striding ahead. 'You don't get ghosts appearing in broad daylight.'

Tom listened to the howling wind and the rain beating down on the roof. He was not so sure. On a day like this, anything and everything seemed possible. Nevertheless, he followed Asa along the corridor. As they approached the door, the squeaking got louder.

'Here goes nothing,' said Asa, as he pushed the door open.

Tom hung back. He was trying to work out what he would do when Asa started screaming for help. He still hadn't decided when he heard him speak.

'Oh, it's you!' said Asa. 'I didn't know you were back early.'

'I neither, until yesterday,' came a voice. The squeaking continued. Tom followed Asa into the gym and looked. A fair-haired girl was sitting on one of the pieces of apparatus, with her feet pressed against a metal rest: by pushing her legs in and out, she was creaking the weights up and down. 'Daddy suddenly announced that he had an important business conference in Buenos Aires, and that was that.' She looked at Tom. 'Hello,' she said. 'I'm Eva. Eva Baumgartner.'

'Tom Selkirk,' said Tom. He was relieved to hear that Eva had arrived that morning: it meant that no fallen trees had cut them off after all. He looked at her. 'You're . . . you're not English, are you?'

Eva laughed. 'You can hear my accent? I'm Swiss. Usually it is English girls who are sent to finishing schools in Switzerland,' she went on. 'I, on the other side, have finished up here!'

'Eva's another *sad*,' Asa explained to Tom. 'Aren't you, Eva?'

The girl shrugged bravely. 'Daddy is a very busy man,' she said, and let her legs relax. The weights came to a rest with a soft clank. 'Yes,' she said softly. 'Maybe too busy.' She stood up and wrapped her towel around her shoulders. 'Anyway, I have to do. I see you later, Asa, Tom.'

As Eva was leaving, Asa called out to her, 'Now you're back, why don't the three of us have a little *celebration*?' he said, loading the word with meaning. 'This evening. Try and do a bit of *shopping*,' he added, and Tom noticed him wink.

Eva smiled. 'A good idea,' she said. 'I'll see what I can do.' And she winked back.

'What was that all about?' Tom asked when Eva had gone.

But Asa wouldn't tell him. 'It's a surprise — that's all I'm going to say,' he said, and Tom understood his new friend well enough by now to know that he meant it.

Suspended from the ceiling in the far corner of the gym was a punch-bag. Asa selected a pair of gloves from the rack. 'Do me up,' he said, and held out his hands for Tom to tie the laces.

At the punch-bag, Asa raised his arms protectively and began bouncing around, throwing punch after punch at the heavy bag. The air was filled with the sound of muffled thuds as the glove pounded against the leather again and again.

Jab with the left. Jab with the left. Jab with

the left. One-two – leading with the right. One-two – leading with the right. Jab with the left. Jab with the right. *Boom-boom-boom-boom-boom*: five body blows in rapid succession.

Tom watched, fascinated. There was something mechanical yet fluid about the movements. As one glove attacked, the other was raised automatically to protect the face – and all the while, the dancing footwork continued.

'Want to put some gloves on?' Asa said, a little breathlessly. 'Go on. There's some your size over there.'

Tom did not particularly want to put on the gloves; boxing had never interested him. However, neither did he want Asa to think he was soft. It was this second consideration that made him walk over to the rack and find a pair of gloves that fitted. As he came to tying the second lace, he realized he had the perfect excuse for going no further.

'I'll have a go when there's someone who can do up both gloves,' he said.

Asa laughed. 'OK,' he said. Tom knew that Asa thought he was chickening out. 'Tomorrow,' he said. 'Eva can lace us up.'

'Fine,' said Tom, trying his best to sound eager. 'Look, I think I'll have a walk round the grounds,' he said. 'See what's there. Pick up some rubbish. Do you fancy coming?'

'In this rain?' said Asa. 'You must be joking!'

Tom turned. 'I'll see you later then.'

To Tom's surprise, neither Asa nor Eva were in the dining hall for dinner that evening. When he questioned Mrs Baxter, she explained that they had both been excused: Asa, because of his continuing stomach upset, and Eva 'for different reasons,' she said vaguely.

'I see,' said Tom. Not that he did. After all, Asa hadn't had a stomach-ache in the first place. What was more, not only had he left half his breakfast, but the packed lunch Mrs Baxter had provided at midday had been left untouched. Tom knew that Asa – who ate like a horse – must be completely famished by now. So where was he?

Tom suspected that Asa was sulking about what had happened in the gym earlier. He'd thought about the whole incident while he was inspecting the grounds – the chapel, the tennis courts and football pitch, the duck pond.

It wasn't that he had been frightened of being useless; or of Asa laughing at him – or even of being hurt. The reason Tom hadn't wanted to put on the gloves was quite different. He was afraid that once he started hitting out, he would be unable to stop. He was afraid that the burning anger inside him would be unleashed. In short, Tom was afraid of losing control.

He laid his spoon down. The gooey chocolate pudding with butterscotch cream was as delicious as it sounded, but Tom could eat no more.

'Are you sure now?' Mrs Baxter asked coaxingly.

Tom nodded. 'It was fantastic,' he said. He got up from his chair. 'I'll go and see if Asa's OK,' he said. 'He's probably up in the dorm.'

'All right then, Tom,' said Mrs Baxter. 'If you're absolutely positive I can't tempt you with any more . . .'

Tom smiled. He'd have to take up boxing just to keep his weight down.

Asa *was* up in the dormitory. He was lying on his bed reading some kind of sci-fi comic book. He looked up as Tom walked in. 'Hiya,' he said. 'Where were you this afternoon? I was looking for you.'

'Were you?' said Tom, and felt guilty for thinking that Asa had been sulking. He realized that Asa Martin simply wasn't the type of boy who did sulk. 'I went back to the library,' Tom explained.

'Did you find anything?' said Asa.

Tom shook his head. 'Not a sausage.'

Asa jumped up from his bed. 'Never mind,' he said. 'Do you fancy a game of cards? Whist, rummy, pontoon . . . You do play cards, I take it?'

'Yes, I do,' Tom laughed. 'Have you ever played Racing Demons? You need two packs.'

'Racing Demons?' Asa grinned. 'You are talking to the undisputed Styles Grange champion of Racing Demons.'

'You haven't played me yet,' said Tom.

'Whoah! A challenge,' said Asa. 'Right, you're on!'

Asa was good at the game. But so, too, was Tom. By the time lights-out arrived at nine-thirty, the score was eleven games all.

'You've got good reactions,' Asa said, as he climbed into his bed. 'That's what you need for boxing.'

Tom smiled to himself: Asa had a one-track mind. There was no way he was ever going to get out of their appointment in the gym. 'Yeah, well, we'll see tomorrow,' he said. 'N'night, Asa.'

'Yeah, night, Tom,' came the reply. 'And . . . sleep well,' he added uncertainly.

Tom knew that Asa was thinking about the hand. He shuddered, and pulled the quilt high over his shoulders. 'You, too,' he said.

Hand or no hand, nothing could have kept Tom awake that night. No sooner had he rolled over on to his favourite side, than he was fast asleep.

It seemed like only minutes later when he was abruptly reawoken. He opened his eyes. It was pitch black. A hideous, rasping squeal was echoing round the room. Then Tom felt something soft brushing across his chin.

58

Suddenly, he was unable to take any more. He opened his mouth and screamed in blind terror.

'Aaarr . . .'

Almost at once, Tom's cries were stifled by a hand which clamped itself firmly over his mouth. He struggled furiously, desperate to break free, but the hand simply tightened its grip. Clearly, it had no intention of letting go.

6

THE UNINVITED GUEST

The hand continued to dig painfully into Tom's cheeks. He was so frightened that he couldn't tell whether the noise, which was still rasping, was in the room or in his head. He reached up and began tearing at the hand, wrenching back the fingers, one by one.

Suddenly, as the hand shifted position, he noticed something which surprised him. The hand was attached to an arm which, in turn, was attached to a body.

'Shut up,' Asa hissed in his ear. 'I'm going to take my hand away, but don't scream.'

The next moment, Tom felt the hand releasing its grip. Asa ran back to his bed. When the rasping squeal came to an abrupt stop, Tom realized that the noise had been caused by Asa's alarm clock – but why was it going off in the middle of the night? 'What's going on?' he said, angrily.

'Sssh!' said Asa. He cocked his head to one side and listened. The sound of distant snoring rumbled in at the far end of the corridor. 'It's all right,' he said finally. 'He's still asleep.'

'Who?' said Tom.

'Mr B,' said Asa. 'The Baxters have got a room in the middle of the corridor that they have to use in the holiday. To keep an eye on us.' He grinned. 'Luckily, Mr Baxter would sleep through a nuclear attack! And Mrs Baxter uses ear-plugs to shut out "her Clifford's" snoring. Now, put your dressing-gown on,' said Asa.

Tom peered into the darkness. He could just make out his friend putting on his own dressing-gown.

'So, where are we going?' said Tom.

Asa turned away. 'Just hurry up,' he said impatiently.

Tom followed Asa along the strip of carpet which led to the door. Then, having checked that the coast was clear, the two boys slipped quietly out of their dormitory, along the corridor, past the Baxters' room, through the fire-door and into the girls' half. At the second door, Asa stopped and knocked softly. Tom heard a rustling sound from inside the room, followed by a girl's voice.

61

'Come,' it said.

They walked in, and there was Eva sitting cross-legged on her bed. Her face was glowing in the flickering light of the candle on her cabinet. On the floor in front of her was a blanket – and on *that* was the most delicious spread of food Tom thought he had ever seen. There were apples, bananas, raisins and dried apricots, crisps and cheesy biscuits, slices of pork pie and legs of chicken, eclairs, doughnuts, cream meringues . . . More important for Tom, were the things that *weren't* there. No boring sandwiches or stodgy fruit-cake; no lettuce or cucumber or tomatoes. Tom hated salad. What was more, the whole wonderful spread was in his honour.

'Surprise!' Asa and Eva called out in unison.

Tom grinned. 'What . . . I . . .' he began. 'A midnight feast. I don't know what to say.'

'Just tuck in then,' said Asa.

'We always make the first one a surprise,' Eva explained, as she poured cola into three glasses.

'But where's it all come from?' said Tom.

Asa and Eva looked at one another and sniggered. 'We clubbed together for the cakes,' said Eva. 'I got them down in the village.'

'But most of it came courtesy of Mrs B,' said Asa with a grin.

'She *gave* you stuff for a midnight feast?' said Tom.

'Yeah. Well, not exactly.'

'You mean you stole it,' said Tom.

"Course we didn't steal it,' said Asa. He paused. 'No, you couldn't call it stealing. The way I look at it is this. Our parents fork out masses to send us here, right?' He shrugged. 'We're just making sure they get value for money.'

Tom laughed.

'Anyway,' Asa went on. 'You heard what she said about the thermostat. If we don't eat it, it'll only go to waste – we're doing everyone a favour!'

'OK,' said Tom. 'You've convinced me.' He looked round at all the food, wondering where to start. 'I wish I hadn't had so much dinner earlier,' he said.

'What was for pud?' Asa asked.

'Gooey Chocolate Pud,' said Tom, 'with . . .'

'. . . butterscotch cream,' said Asa. 'Blast! I forgot – was there any left?'

'Yeah,' said Tom. 'Loads.'

Asa grinned. 'I'll be two minutes,' he said, and with that, he was off.

With Asa gone, the atmosphere altered. Tom remembered his friend's theory about *glads* and *sads*. He was sure that it wasn't that simple, and yet he couldn't help noticing how his mood had changed. When he was with Asa, he would pretend to be happier than he really was; just so that they could get along. With Eva – another *sad* – he no longer needed to make the effort. As they talked, it wasn't long before they were swapping stories about how unfair it was that they'd been sent away.

Tom told Eva all about Mr Selkirk's new job in Singapore, and about his time at Mallowbury, and about that feeling you get in the pit of your stomach when the time for farewells comes round *again*! And Eva told him about *her* family: how her mother had died when she was little; how her father – unable to cope – had sent her and her brother off to boarding school, so that he could lose himself in his career.

'Does your brother come here, too?' said Tom.

'He was here before,' said Eva. 'But he is seven years older than I. He has a job now – also in Switzerland,' she added, and sighed.

Tom sighed with her. 'One day, *we'll* be able to leave this place, too,' he said.

Meanwhile, at the bottom of the stairs, Asa had paused to get his bearings. He wanted to end up in the kitchen – not tumbling down the basement stairs which lay behind the adjacent door.

Taking care not to make a sound, he tiptoed across the hall, checked that he was at the correct door, and quickly went inside. The whole kitchen – steel worktops, white wall tiles and all – was bathed in the purple glow of the electric fly-ring above the cooker.

The cold-room was on the opposite side of the

kitchen. Asa walked up to the heavy white door and pressed the light switch on the wall next to it. Then, taking hold of the handle, he heaved the door open. The light from inside fanned out across the floor.

Asa nipped in. He knew he had five minutes before the timer switch turned itself off; five minutes to find the remains of Mrs Baxter's fantastic chocolate and butterscotch pudding. He hoped he'd have a bit more luck here than in the library.

'Yeah!' he cried as, a short while later, he hit the jackpot. There, on the middle shelf at the far end of the cool-room was the pudding in question. What was more, there was – as Tom had said – loads of it. Asa grinned, picked up the dish and made his way back to the door.

The next instant, he stopped. He stared ahead of him, scarcely daring to breathe. Suspended in mid-air by the door was the hand. Outside, the chapel bell was chiming.

If I can just get past without it noticing, thought Asa. After all, a hand can't see, can it?

Unfortunately, this was only half true. For, although the hand had no eyes, it could 'see' just as well as Asa. Better, in fact. By sensing each and every tiny movement of the air, it did not need light to find its way around.

Asa crept towards the door, step after trembling step. The hand remained motionless; the bell continued to chime – but impossibly slowly now. It was as if time itself had turned to slow-motion.

All at once, everything changed. As Asa reached the door and was about to duck down underneath the hand, it suddenly formed itself into a fist and rapped him sharply on the head.

'OW!' Asa cried, and looked up in surprise.

This was a mistake. Before he had a chance to move, the hand opened up and slapped him – once, twice – hard across both cheeks.

'Stop!' Asa yelled. 'Leave me alone.'

The hand did stop, but it hadn't finished yet. First of all, it dipped one bony finger into the chocolate pudding. Then, with all its fingers outstretched, it lunged forwards and shoved the boy viciously in the chest.

Asa flew backwards into the cool-room and fell crashing to the floor. As he landed, the dish slipped from his fingers. Somehow, it managed to turn itself upside down in mid-flight. When Asa opened his eyes he found all the remains of the Gooey Chocolate Pud and butterscotch sauce in his lap. It seeped through his pyjamas, cold and claggy.

'Oh, what?' he groaned, and was just trying to scrape the sticky brown mess back into the bowl when the door slammed shut. 'NO!' he yelled.

He leapt to his feet and ran towards the door.

Then, just as he got there, the light went out. 'LET ME OUT! LET ME OUT!' he screamed, and pummelled frantically at the door. 'Please let me out!'

'And the problem will not go away,' Eva was saying, above the sound of the chiming bell. 'I said to my daddy, "If you loved me you would not send me away to school." Then he says, "It is *because* I love you that I send you away."'

Tom nodded. It was all so familiar.

'And then he says, "And if you loved *me* you would go to school happily; you would not always make such a . . ."'

Suddenly, she stopped. Tom realized that she was staring at something behind him. 'What is it?' he asked anxiously.

But Eva didn't reply. From the look on her face, Tom knew she was staring at something terrifying, something ghoulish – he knew that the hand was there again.

Slowly, he turned his head until he was staring right behind him. And there it was . . . Over by the door . . .

The severed hand!

As if Tom's turning round had been a signal, the hand clenched itself into a fist and flew through the air towards him. Arms raised in defence, Tom tried to keep it away from

67

his face. But it was no use. The hand was too fast. Weaving and diving, it jabbed at him without any warning.

Time and again, it made contact with Tom's jaw. The odd thing was, the punches did not hurt. It was as if the hand was playing with him; sparring. As if . . .

'Asa!' Tom cried.

As he cried out, so the hand flew away from him. It paused in mid-air and curled itself up – all except for the index finger, which wagged at them. What did it mean? Tom wondered. *Beware* perhaps; or *that'll teach you* – or possibly, *pay attention*. Suddenly, the hand was off again. It flew to the window and, with the index finger still extended, began running its nail, squeaking and scratching, over the glass.

'Writing,' Eva gasped. 'I think it's writing something.'

As abruptly as it had begun, so the hand also stopped. It turned, waved, and – as the final stroke of midnight echoed away to nothing – it disappeared.

Eva and Tom leapt up and raced towards the window. There, in the condensation on the glass, was a word and a number. At least, that was what it most looked like. The letters were so childishly formed that it was difficult to tell for sure.

'Storm 9,' said Tom. He looked at Eva. 'Does that mean anything to you?'

Eva shook her head. 'Nothing,' she said. 'It didn't write anything before.'

'Before!' Tom exclaimed.

'At the beginning of the holiday,' Eva explained. 'Daddy was late picking me up. I saw it two times – twice – but it just ran around on the floor. Nothing like this,' she said, looking back at the window.

'Storm 9,' Tom said again. 'Perhaps it's some kind of message. Look at the way it's been written,' he added. 'S T O, then a gap, then the R; and then another gap before the M.'

Eva snorted. 'You try writing with your eyes closed,' she said.

'Good point,' said Tom. 'The thing is . . .'

Just then, Tom's thoughts were interrupted by the distant sound of muffled banging. 'What the . . .' he muttered. He remembered his friend. 'Asa!' Tom cried for a second time. 'He's in trouble. I know he is. Come on.'

The banging got louder as Tom and Eva raced down the stairs. By the time they got to the bottom, they realized that the noise was indeed coming from the kitchen. Tom sped across the hallway and pushed open the door.

'NOT THAT ONE!' Eva shouted at him. Tom skidded to a halt. With thumping heart, he looked into the shadowy darkness of the stairs he had almost tumbled down. 'They lead to the basement,' she explained. 'This is the kitchen door.'

69

Together, they went inside. Like Asa, they were immediately struck by the eerie purple light. It drained their faces of all colour, making them look sunken-eyed and deathly pale. Suddenly, Eva cried out again. 'Look!' she yelled.

Tom followed the line of her pointing finger, and there – in crude brown letters on the door of the cool-room – was the message again. STORM 9.

Without a moment's hesitation, both Eva and Tom ran over to the cool-room. Tom removed the skewer which had been jammed into the lock, and pulled the door open. As he did so, Asa fell forwards and collapsed on the tiled floor beside him.

'Are you all right?' Eva said, and crouched down next to him. 'Asa? Are you OK?'

Asa looked up wearily. 'C . . . c . . . cold,' he said.

'Come with me,' said Eva, helping him to his feet. 'Hey,' she said. 'You're covered in chocolate.'

'I . . . I . . . I know,' Asa shuddered. 'It . . . it . . . the hand!' he said.

'I'll see to the mess,' said Tom. 'You two go on up. I'll be with you in a minute.'

Although Tom did not want to be left alone, he could see that his friend wasn't going to be much help until he warmed up a bit. When Asa and Eva left, he took a mop and a bucket from the corner and swabbed the floor of the cold-room clean. He shivered. If this is how cold it is when the thermostat's broken, Asa was lucky, he thought. Otherwise, he could be dead now.

He poured the dirty water down the sink, and rinsed the mop.

'But then, if the hand *was* trying to kill Asa, why did it lead us to him?'

Confused, Tom picked up a dishcloth and returned to the door. He stared at the letters, smeared onto the white surface with the sticky chocolate sauce. The spacing of the letters was the same as on the window. STO R M 9.

Perhaps it wasn't an accident, after all, he thought. Perhaps the hand meant to write it like that. But why? With one sweep of the cloth, he wiped the mysterious message away. 'It makes no sense,' he muttered irritably. 'Unless . . .'

Tom chucked the dishcloth into a nearby sink and raced back up the stairs. He found Eva and Asa in the boys' dorm. Asa was sitting on his bed, wrapped up in his quilt.

'Quick,' said Tom. 'Help me with the bed, Eva.'

Eva didn't stop to ask why. With her at the side, and Tom at the back, the pair of them pulled Tom's bed away from the wall. 'That should do it,' said Tom. 'Yes!' he exclaimed a moment later. 'Just as I thought!'

He and Eva looked down; Asa came to join them. Together, the three of them read the message written in the dust.

STO R M 9.

'But how did you know?' said Eva.

'Last night – when I first saw the hand,' he explained, 'I heard it scratching at something under the bed. I didn't think of looking then . . .'

Asa shrugged. 'So what?' he said. 'It's the same message – and now we know it means the cool-room. Eva told me how you found me so quick.'

'Yes, but don't you see,' said Tom. 'It was written last night – before you'd even thought of having the midnight feast.'

'Yes, but . . .'

'Let's go through what happened,' said Tom firmly. 'Last night, the hand tried to warn us that something was going to happen. Then tonight something *did* happen – Asa was locked in the cool-room. The question is, why would the hand tell us what it was going to do? And why, having locked you in, did it then help us to find you?'

'That's two questions,' said Asa grumpily.

'*I* don't think it was trying to harm you at all,' said Tom, scratching his head thoughtfully.

'You could've fooled me,' said Asa.

'I think,' Tom went on, 'that it could have happened to any of us. I think yesterday's message was the hand's attempt to tell us something important. And I think tonight's message was a second and third attempt to tell us the same thing. It is trying to make us go somewhere, but . . .' He paused. 'Not the cool-room itself. Though maybe somewhere similar.'

'Then why pick the cool-room in the first place?' Asa persisted.

'Because that's where you happened to be at the stroke of midnight,' said Tom. 'Didn't you notice the bells again? It's obvious. The hand only appears when the chapel bell is chiming twelve midnight. And that's not very long, is it? Twenty-five . . . thirty seconds at the most. That's all the time it's got to communicate . . . to communicate whatever it is it wants to communicate . . .'

'And what's that?' said Asa.

Tom shrugged. 'I don't know,' he admitted. 'But I'll tell you what: I don't think the hand is going to go away until we do know.'

7

STORM 9

Tom slept surprisingly well that night. In all the excitement, neither he nor Asa had remembered to close the dormitory curtains, and when he finally woke up, bright sunlight was streaming into the room.

Tom sat up, rubbed his eyes and looked over at Asa's bed. To his surprise, he saw that it was empty. He assumed that Asa must be in the bathroom.

When he still hadn't returned fifteen minutes later, however, Tom got up. It was then that he noticed the note lying on Asa's pillow.

Tom, it said,
Couldn't stop thinking about what you said

*last night. I think you may be right. If the
cool-room was the place the hand wanted us
to go, then I would have seen something –
and I didn't.*

*I've thought of a place that STORM 9
might be, and I'm going to investigate.
Lucky Miss Bennett cancelled the Morning
Meeting. Meet me in the gym at 11. I'll tell
you everything then.*

Asa.

p.s. Bring your P.E. kit.

Tom smiled. In spite of all the business with
the hand, Asa still hadn't forgotten about the
boxing.

Having washed and dressed, Tom went down
to breakfast. Once again, he was the only one
there. Mrs Baxter told him that both Asa and
Eva had been and gone over an hour earlier.

'They both seemed a bit agitated,' she said,
and stared questioningly at the boy. Tom
guessed that she was fishing for information.
She was going to be disappointed. Tom was not
about to tell her what was happening. After all,
if the hand had wanted to communicate with
her, it would have done so.

'Did they?' he said. 'I wonder why.'

Mrs Baxter continued to stare at him. 'You
don't know, then?' she said.

''Fraid not,' said Tom and, feeling his cheeks red-
den, he turned his attention to his poached eggs.

He heard Mrs Baxter making a *hmmph* noise as she left the room. He lay down his knife and fork, and sighed with relief. Tom didn't like lying at the best of times; with Mrs Baxter – who was being so nice to him – it seemed particularly unfair. Yet Tom was sure he had made the right decision. Whatever was going on at Styles Grange, it concerned only the children.

He picked up his cutlery again, and made a half-hearted attempt on his meal. Not that he was hungry – the midnight feast had seen to that. Two mouthfuls later, he admitted defeat and pushed the knife and fork together on his plate. Then, unable to face Mrs Baxter with another unfinished breakfast, he slipped quietly away.

As he made his way back upstairs, Tom wondered what to do. It was only nine o'clock, so he had two hours to kill before meeting up with Asa. As he got to the first floor, he thought that he really should check out the library again. The book must be there somewhere. But just the thought of all those packed shelves was enough to put him off.

'Later,' he muttered, as he continued upwards.

At the second floor, he wondered whether it wouldn't be a good idea to try to discover STORM 9 for himself. After all, there was no guarantee that Asa's hunch would prove to be correct. Then again, he had no idea where to start. Perhaps, though, the fact that the hand had appeared first in the dormitories was important. Perhaps the mysterious STORM 9 was situated there.

As Tom continued up the stairs, however, he was conscious that he was becoming increasingly nervous. His stomach felt fluttery; his pulse was beginning to race – he felt dizzy. With every step, his fear increased until, by the time he reached the third-floor landing, he had to grip the banister to remain upright. He closed his eyes and tried to still the dreadful swirling motion that seemed to be spiralling up from his stomach to his head.

With his hands on his hips, Tom took three deep breaths, and stood up straight. He opened his eyes. The whirling sensation had gone – but his heart was beating faster than ever. He looked round anxiously.

Ahead of him was the corridor. Without knowing why, Tom found himself walking along it. On either side were the classrooms he had looked in on with Asa. This time, though, Tom did not stop. Instead, he continued to the very end. There, he saw something that he hadn't noticed the day before: a second, smaller corridor, at right-angles to the first.

With his heart in his mouth, Tom turned into the narrow passageway and kept walking. The left-hand wall was covered with sepia photographs of cricket XIs and rugby XVs; the right-hand wall was lined with doors. Tom tried the first one. It was locked. The second, however, opened to reveal a stock-room full of dusty sets of books. The third was also locked; as was the fourth – but in the fifth, the shelves were packed with old sports gear: cricket pads, footballs, rackets that needed restringing, a broken javelin. *And* an old pair of boxing gloves, Tom noted miserably. He closed the door and went on.

At the end of the corridor was a window. The sun was streaming through in a dazzling wedge which, as Tom reached the sixth door, made him squint. It, too, was locked; and so was the seventh. Door number eight, however, was open. Tom went inside. As he opened the door, dust flew up like glittering sparks into the sunlight.

The room was full of costumes and props from countless school plays. There were gowns and crowns, suits and boots, vases, blankets, candlesticks, ropes, spades, swords – all manner of objects, each one neatly labelled with the title of the play and the year it was used. Tom picked up a policeman's helmet, blew off the dust, put it on his head and inspected himself in the mirror.

"Ello, 'ello, 'ello,' he said, and grinned at his reflection. 'And tell me, sir, where were you on the night of the fifth?' He put the helmet back on the shelf. Whatever he was looking for, he knew it was not here – and yet, although he couldn't tell why, he sensed that *something* was still urging him on.

Tom returned to the narrow corridor and closed the door behind him. As he did so, he felt tingles of nervous anticipation running up and down his spine. He was getting close. Horribly close.

Wincing into the brightness of the sun, he looked up at the final door. Like all the others, it bore a small plaque with the name of the room on it: in this case, *Storeroom 9*. As he stared at it, his heart missed a beat.

Some of the brass letters were old, some were more modern replacements. The newer letters glinted in the sunlight – an R, the E and the two Os. The rest were duller, though none the less spectacular for that, for they spelled out the message that Tom had been searching for. Even the gaps were in the right places.

STO R M 9.

Tom tried to steady his shaking hand as he reached out for the door handle. Would the door be open, or were the contents of the room to remain a mystery? Slowly, he lowered the handle and pushed gently on the door with his shoulder. It did not budge. Hoping against hope that he had simply not pushed hard enough, he had another go.

The next instant, he let out a scream of terror which echoed back down the passage, along the corridor and out into the cavernous stairwell. 'NOOOOoooooooo!!' Something hard, cold and bony had seized hold of his right ear and was twisting it. Tom screamed again; this time, in pain. 'Let go of me!' he cried.

But the hand would not let go. Its pincer-like fingers twisted viciously round, pulling Tom off-balance. Now that the hand had caught its quarry, it seemed in no mood to release it in a hurry.

'Help,' Tom whimpered, as he found himself falling backwards. So much for his theory that the hand could only appear when the bells were chiming midnight. The hand, he now realized, could manifest itself whenever it wanted – and there was nothing he could do to make it go away.

'Help me,' he cried weakly. 'Please.'

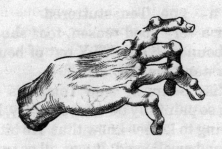

8

OUT OF BOUNDS

As he landed on the ground with a thud, Tom suddenly saw that there was more to the hand than he had thought. Heavy brown shoes, for a start; then lumpy legs wrapped in woolly tights, and a tartan skirt that started just below the knee and went up to a black belt around a plump waist. As Tom continued his upward gaze, he found himself staring into Miss Bennett's face. Her pale blue eyes glared at him icily.

'Thomas Selkirk,' she said. 'Stand up, please.'

Tom did as he was told, and stood in front of her, head bowed.

'Did Asa show you around here yesterday?' she said, her voice little more than a whisper. 'Well, did he?'

'No . . . n . . . no,' Tom stuttered.

'And for a very good reason, too,' she said. 'It is out of bounds, STRICTLY out of bounds. Do you understand me? DO YOU?'

'Yes, Miss Bennett,' said Tom. His ear was throbbing so painfully he wanted to cry. Not that he was going to let *her* know that. He bit into his lower lip and swallowed. It was all so unfair! He hadn't *meant* to do anything wrong.

'I can see I'm going to have to keep my eye on you,' Miss Bennett was saying. 'Now be off with you. Next time I won't be so lenient. Do you understand me?'

'Yes, Miss Bennett,' Tom said. He did understand. He understood that if he did *anything* to arouse Miss Bennett's suspicions again, he would be for it. The problem was, how else was he going to get to the bottom of the mystery of the severed hand?

Tom turned and left. As he walked along the corridor, he was sure he could feel those ice-cold eyes of hers boring into the back of his head. It was only when he turned right at the end and started trotting down the stairs that the pounding of his heart finally began to slow.

As he reached the final flight of stairs, Tom heard a voice calling up to him. 'Watcha!' it said.

It was Asa, standing by the front door. 'Hiya,' he said.

'Are you all right?' said Asa, as he watched

Tom coming towards him. 'You look as if you've seen a ghost.'

Tom smiled weakly. 'Worse,' he said. 'Far worse. But we can't talk here,' he added, and looked around furtively. 'Let's go for a walk.'

It was still sunny outside. The ferocious storms had been followed by a spell of good weather. Not that it was going to last: the long-range weather forecast was for even worse weather to come.

'So what's going on?' said Asa, as they walked across the grass.

'You first,' said Tom. 'You left me that note.'

Asa snorted. 'Waste of time,' he said. 'I thought the hand might be trying to lead us to the weather box.'

'Weather box?' said Tom.

'You know, that white beehive thing at the back of the school,' he said. 'It's got a thermometer on it, and a barometer, and a gauge for measuring rainfall. *Storm – weather*. I thought there might be a connection.' Tom nodded. 'But there was nothing there,' he went on. 'What about you?'

Tom stopped. He turned and looked at his friend. 'I've found out exactly what STORM 9 means,' he said. 'And where it is.'

'You have!' Asa exclaimed. 'Where?'

And Tom told him. With his eyes fixed grimly on the grass at his feet, he told him everything:

about the corridor with the row of storerooms, about the mixture of old and new letters on door number nine, about the hand which was not *the* hand – and about Miss Bennett's veiled warning. Only when he finished did Tom look up.

The expression on Asa's face was one of admiration and sympathy. He breathed in sharply through this teeth. 'Tricky,' he said. Then he grinned. 'Still, we're not going to let Miss Bennett stand in our way, are we?'

'The thing is,' Tom said doubtfully, 'the door was locked and . . .'

'No problem,' said Asa. 'There are two sets of school keys. Miss Bennett's got one lot – but they might prove a bit difficult to get hold of! The second set though should be a cinch.'

'You know where they are?' said Tom.

Asa nodded. 'Mr B's got them,' he said.

'Mr Baxter?' said Tom.

'The very same,' said Asa, and laughed. 'He's not just a baby-sitter. He's been working on that broken boiler ever since you arrived,' Asa went on. 'And with a bit of luck, that's where we'll find him now – down in the boiler-room. Come on, let's go.'

For a second, Tom held back. He didn't want Miss Bennett on his back again – or twisting his ear round, come to that. Then again, he also knew that the hand wouldn't let itself be ignored. Like it or not, if Tom ever wanted to sleep soundly at Styles Grange, he would have to solve the mystery of the hand once and for all. And if that meant breaking into Storeroom 9, then so be it. He'd just have to make sure he wasn't caught.

Asa turned round. 'Are you coming or not?' he said.

'Yes,' said Tom wearily. 'I'm coming.'

9

DOWN IN THE BASEMENT

The way to the boiler-room was through the door next to the kitchen, and down a flight of stairs – the stairs Tom had almost fallen down the previous night. Having checked that there was nobody about, Asa and Tom slipped through.

As they went down the dark, concrete steps, Tom noticed the temperature increasing. The boiler-room, it seemed, was the one warm place in the whole of the school. And, as Asa pushed open the door at the bottom of the stairs, they were both struck by a blast of hot, oily air.

They walked in and Tom looked round. Despite all the metal pipes and heavy machinery, the basement room was cosy. The ceiling was low, and the blazing furnace bathed everything in a warm orange light. What was more, the whole place was full of personal belongings.

There were family photographs fixed to the cupboard doors with sticky tape, there were crayon drawings addressed 'to Grandpa' propped up on the shelves, and countless bits and pieces that must have been given by those same grandchildren – shells and pretty stones, conkers on strings, and painted clay objects that might have been animals.

And over by the pump, with a spanner in his hand, was Mr Baxter himself. Dressed only in a set of blue overalls, he was crouching down, and muttering to himself. Asa coughed. 'Morning, Mr B,' he said.

The man looked round. Like his wife, he too had thick grey hair, a round, red face and smiley blue eyes. They might have been twins. 'Asa,' he said, as he pulled himself up. 'And someone new.'

'This is Tom Selkirk,' said Asa.

Mr Baxter crossed the floor, wiped his greasy hand on the back of his overalls and held it out to Tom. 'Pleased to meet you,' he said.

Tom smiled back. He liked the old man immediately.

'Now then,' said Mr Baxter, checking his watch. 'Time for a spot of elevenses, I'd say. Would you care to join me in a mug of tea?'

'That would be great,' said Asa and, when Mr

Baxter went to fill up the kettle, he turned to Tom and winked. Then he nodded towards the jacket hanging up behind the door. 'OK?' he whispered.

'OK,' Tom mouthed back.

Asa and Tom had planned what they were going to do on the way there. Asa's job was to get Mr Baxter into some kind of conversation – something that would distract him. Then, while his back was turned, Tom was to take the relevant key from the bunch which was kept, on a chain, in the top left pocket of his jacket. It had sounded easy. Now, Tom was not so sure. For a start, the jacket was hanging in full view of most of the room. And when Asa started talking – well, Tom thought that he was about to give the whole game away.

'Mr B?' he said, brightly. 'Is Styles Grange haunted?'

To Tom's surprise, Mr Baxter threw back his head and roared with laughter. 'Haunted!' he said. 'Now who's been putting silly ideas like that into your head, eh?'

'No-one,' said Asa. 'Only . . .'

'I suppose you've been hearing tales of the old prospectus, haven't you?' said Mr Baxter.

Asa and Tom nodded. They hadn't, but it sounded interesting.

'Back in 'seventy-six, it was. 'Seventy-six/seventy-seven,' he went on. 'I remember at

88

the time thinking what a daft idea it was. Still, some people won't be told.'

Asa shook his head earnestly. 'Remind me what happened exactly,' he said.

'Ah, well,' said Mr Baxter. 'You'll remember how it all started. That boy – what was his name, now? *Jake* something. Jake Armitage, that was it. 'Course, in those days, it was all boys – and English boys at that. Funny,' he added. 'If it hadn't been for the so-called ghost, I suppose it still would be.' The kettle boiled. 'There you are, lads,' he said a minute later as he set down the two steaming mugs of tea in front of them. 'Now, where was I?'

'So-called ghosts,' said Asa.

Mr Baxter chuckled. 'Hysteria, more like,' he said. 'All those lonely boys missing their mums and dads – and grandmas and grandpas, I shouldn't wonder.' He lowered his voice. 'I know I work here,' he said, 'but I can't say as I like the idea of boarding schools. A child needs his family.'

Tom heard Asa snorting beside him. He knew what his friend – as a *glad* – was thinking. Mr Baxter, on the other hand, noticed nothing. His eyes glazed over as, cupping the mug in his hands, he returned to the series of events which had started in 1976.

Apparently, Jake Armitage had gone to see Matron complaining that he couldn't sleep.

Further investigations revealed that he was suffering from nightmares – or rather, night *visions*. Every night, or so he claimed, he was woken up at midnight by a kind of ghost . . .

Tom and Asa tried hard not to let any emotion show on their faces as Mr Baxter went on to explain precisely *what* kind of ghost it had been.

'A hand,' he said. 'A severed hand!' And he described how increasing numbers of boys claimed to see the hand as well – 'although, oddly enough, it always refused to appear whenever a member of staff spent the night in the dormitory with them,' he added, and laughed. 'Hysteria, you see,' he said, looking at Tom. 'Mass hysteria.'

Tom nodded, but he remained unconvinced. If the hand was just the result of homesickness, then why had Asa seen it? He *hated* being at home. It didn't make sense.

'Things would probably have blown over,' Mr Baxter was saying, 'if it hadn't been for the by-pass scheme.'

The by-pass, it turned out, was the local council's attempt to ease the traffic problem in the centre of town. If it had gone ahead, the proposed road would have cut off the north-western corner of the Styles Grange estate. This would have meant demolishing the chapel. The then headteacher – a Mr Lionel Luscombe – was furious, and immediately launched a vigorous campaign to scupper the proposals. And when he heard the tales of a ghostly hand which haunted the dormitories at midnight, Mr Luscombe – a resourceful man – decided to make use of them.

He wrote letters to the press, he appeared on radio and TV programmes, he published a paper entitled *Restless Spirits*. He made it clear that he felt the ghost had appeared to prevent the destruction of a part of the estate – *to lend a hand*, so to speak. And he went on to give a sinister warning of the hazards for any drivers who happened to be on that particular stretch of road at the stroke of midnight if the chapel *was* demolished.

With all the publicity came increased opposition to the by-pass proposals. Eager to continue the momentum, Mr Luscombe had a new school prospectus printed. In it, he referred to the mysterious ghost of Styles Grange which was trying to save the school chapel. This time, however, he had gone too far.

'I mean, parents don't want to hear they're sending their kids to a Haunted House, do they?' Mr Baxter reasoned. 'They started to find other schools. Numbers dropped. Teachers left. The whole place was in a dreadful state.'

'So, what happened?' asked Asa.

'Well,' said Mr Baxter, and took a long slurp of tea, 'Mr Luscombe resigned. It seemed a bit unfair at the time – after all, he *had* managed to get the route of the by-pass altered. But there was no way he could have stayed on. So, that's when Dr Buchanan joined us. It was him who opened the place up to girls, and encouraged foreign students to study here. Printed a revised prospectus, he did, as well – one *without* the ghost in it! Numbers picked up again.'

'And the ghost?' said Tom. 'The ghost of the hand?'

'That left, too,' Mr Baxter chortled. 'I often wondered whether the whole thing wasn't set up by Mr Luscombe in the first place.' He drained his mug and placed it down on the table. 'Tell you what, though,' he added, 'I think I may have a copy of that old prospectus somewhere. I wonder where I could have put it?'

He stood up and made his way round to the far corner of the boiler-room. This was the moment the boys had both been waiting for.

While Asa went with him to make sure he didn't return too soon, Tom nipped over to the door. He reached up to the coat on the hook, and felt for the bunch of keys.

And they were there, just where Asa had said they'd be. Taking care not to let them jingle, Tom pulled them slowly from the pocket. Then, with the heavy bunch in his left palm, he began slipping them one by one along the ring. The kitchen key, the gym key, the keys to the laboratories and the classrooms; they were all there, each one neatly labelled.

Storeroom 1 he came to at last, and flicked quickly down through the numbers. *Storeroom 6. Storeroom 7.* And there it was. *Storeroom 9.*

Fingers trembling, Tom forced the little key into the end of the spiral ring and – bit by bit – eased it round. After what seemed like an eternity, the key finally dropped into his hand. Tom breathed a sigh of relief. He returned the bunch of keys to the jacket, slipped the key to the storeroom into his pocket, and hurried back to where Asa and Mr Baxter were standing. Mr Baxter, it seemed, hadn't even noticed his absence.

'You can take it if you like,' he was saying to Asa, and he handed him the copy of the ill-fated prospectus. 'But I'd quite like it back.'

'I'll look after it,' Asa assured him. 'And thanks for the tea.'

'My pleasure,' said Mr Baxter. He sighed. 'I suppose I'd better get back to that wretched boiler. I don't know,' he grumbled. 'All these things breaking down. I'll tell you what, if Styles Grange is haunted, I wouldn't mind if it came to lend *me* a hand!'

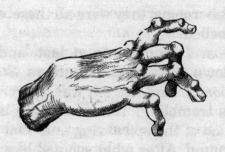

10

THE GRAVESTONE

After the warmth of the boiler-room, the dormitory felt colder than ever. Tom put on another jumper, but it made no difference. The damp chill of Styles Grange had already wormed itself into his bones, and no amount of extra clothing would make it go away.

'It *must* be more than a coincidence,' Asa was saying, as he turned the storeroom key over and over in his hand. 'I mean why should you, me and Eva see the same thing – *exactly* the same thing as those kids did twenty odd years ago?'

'I know,' said Tom excitedly. 'And what's more, we also know *why* the hand is appearing again.'

'We do?' said Asa.

'It's obvious,' said Tom. 'Last time it showed

itself was because Styles Grange was in danger – they were going to knock down part of it for that new road. And what happened as soon as the scheme was dropped? The hand went away again.'

'So?' said Asa.

'Well, it had done what it set out to do, hadn't it? The hand must be . . . I don't know, some kind of guardian. Whenever the school's under threat, it comes back to do something about it.'

Asa looked doubtful. 'It seems a bit far-fetched,' he said.

'Have you got a better idea?' said Tom.

Asa shook his head. He looked at Tom. 'So what you're saying is, the hand has come back again because Styles Grange is in danger now.'

Tom shrugged. 'I know it sounds crazy but . . . I just can't think of any other explanation. Something that we don't know about – something *bad* – is happening here. And we, for whatever reason, are being used to sort it out.'

'But whose hand is it?' said Tom. 'And why does it only appear at midnight? And what *is* in Storeroom 9? Come on,' he said, flicking the key up in the air and catching it again. 'Let's go and have a quick look . . .'

'No way!' said Tom firmly. 'We agreed. We'll check it out after lights-out. Anyway,' he added, 'maybe Eva'll want to come along – maybe she's *meant* to come along.'

'Chicken,' Asa muttered.

'Too right!' said Tom, and he tenderly rubbed at the ear Miss Bennett had tweaked so viciously.

'Yeah, all right,' said Asa. 'I was only joking. So what *do* we do?'

'For a start,' said Tom, 'I think we ought to have a look at that prospectus. Where is it?'

'Oh, yeah,' said Asa. 'I'd forgotten.' He reached into his back pocket and pulled out the little booklet. 'Here we go,' he said.

The two boys sat side by side on Asa's bed, flicking through the pages of the old prospectus. Most of it was the same as the one Tom had looked at with his parents; how long ago that now seemed! But there were differences. Important differences.

In the first place, the STYLES GRANGE SCHOOL PROSPECTUS 1976, as it was called, was thicker than the current edition. Most of the extra pages were taken up with details of the chapel which Mr Luscombe had been so keen to rescue.

'The foundations of this small Roman . . . roman-esque chapel,' Tom read out, *'were originally laid in 1829, although building continued until the late 1850s. Clad in stone, it has an ornately carved west door arch and a truncated "dovecote" south tower . . .'*

'Yeah, yeah,' said Asa impatiently. 'Next!'

Tom turned the page and started reading again. *'Of more interest than the clock, is the bell itself. Cast in bronze at the Josiah Boothroyd Works, Manchester, in 1868, the one-and-a-half ton bell is —'*

'This is boring!' Asa interrupted again. 'Let's turn to the bit about the ghost.'

'It might be boring,' said Tom, 'but it also might be important.'

'How do you mean?' said Asa.

'I'm not sure,' said Tom. 'But . . . well, we know the hand appears when the bell is chiming twelve. Well, what if there's a reason for that? What if the bell and the hand are somehow connected?

Asa looked at his friend and sighed. 'Go on then,' he said grudgingly. 'But not *too* much!' he added.

Tom returned to his place. *'. . . ton bell is . . . is the only one of its kind. The relief design is of a line of animals marching two by two in a never-ending spiral up the outside of the bell, and down the inside. Despite the apparent irregularity of shape, the bell is not only balanced, but it resonates on a perfect B sharp.'*

'Be sharp!' said Asa. 'Ooooooohh!' he wailed spookily. 'It's another message.'

'Idiot,' Tom laughed. He turned the page.

'THE HAND OF STYLES GRANGE,' he read.

'That's more like it!' said Asa. 'Let's have a look.'

Tom moved the prospectus over, so it was directly between the two of them. Together, they read through the story of the mysterious hand. As they did so, their eyes grew large and their mouths dropped open. Not only did it tell them about the hand itself, but Tom was right: there *was* a connection between it and the bell.

Apparently, it was on the fifteenth of March, 1869, and after some considerable delay caused by the inaccessibility of the school – then a private manor-house – that the bell was finally ready to be installed in the chapel tower. A wooden scaffold had been erected inside the tower, and a pulley and rope system set up to raise the heavy bell on to the hook waiting for it under the roof.

The problems continued. One of the horses being used to raise the bell went lame, and there was a freak thunderstorm which made any moving of the bell impossible. In the end, it was gone ten o'clock at night when everyone was finally in place to lift the bell.

As well as the carthorses, which had been hitched together and secured to the main rope, there were some forty men, women and children there to help with the lifting. Positioned all the way up the scaffolding, their job was to steady the bell as it rose up through the air. One of those volunteers was Silas Grimsby.

Silas was a local lad whose mother was employed at Styles Grange as cook. When she died, Wolfgang Geisselhardt – the founder of the manor – had taken pity on the boy and kept him on. He became a sort of jack-of-all-trades; polishing boots, running errands, tending the chickens, helping in the kitchens. When the bell had arrived, Silas, along with most of the other staff of Styles Grange, had been sent up the scaffolding.

The lifting of the bell commenced. At first everything went well. As it reached half-way up the tower, however, something began to happen: the bell began to turn. Eager to be of help, Silas Grimsby leant forward and seized the ropes which were winding themselves around one another.

Suddenly, the whole lot jerked and twisted, and Silas Grimsby was trapped, his wrist crushed between the thick ropes. What happened next is unclear. Perhaps the sheer weight of the bell caused the rope to cut into his flesh; perhaps the twisting snapped his bones. One thing was certain: Silas Grimsby's right hand was severed at the wrist. More gruesome than this, it was never seen again.

*   *   *

'*And it is the spirit of this hand – separated for ever from Silas Grimsby – which roams the grounds of Styles Grange to this day*,' Tom read out, his voice all but inaudible. He closed the prospectus and lay it down on the bed. 'Blimey,' he muttered.

Asa shook his head. 'Can you *imagine* it? Your hand being cut off like that? The splinter of bones, the spurt of blood . . .'

'Yeah, all right,' said Tom, wincing queasily. 'I wonder why they didn't just cut the rope?'

'What, and risk breaking the bell?' said Asa. 'Don't be so naïve.'

Tom nodded glumly. He knew Asa was right. If the choice had really been between damaging the costly bell and injuring the poor orphan, then the hand of Silas Grimsby had never stood a chance. He glanced at his watch. 'Half past three,' he said. 'Why don't we go and have a look at the chapel. See if there's anything interesting there.'

'OK,' said Asa reluctantly. He pulled himself up off the bed.

'You don't have to come,' said Tom.

'No, I want to,' said Asa. 'It's just that I've been to the chapel hundreds of times. I've never noticed anything much before.'

'That's because you didn't know what you were looking for,' said Tom.

For once, the weathermen were right. The

sunny weather of the morning had proved to be the lull before the storm. As they stepped outside, Asa and Tom were struck by the full force of a howling gale. Above them, huge black ridges of cloud tumbled across the sky.

With their heads down, the two boys crossed the playing fields and headed up through the woods towards the chapel. The wind was so strong, it took their breath away. The long grass rippled like water. Fallen leaves were whipped up off the ground and swirled through the air like a swarm of locusts. The deciduous trees twisted this way and that, their leafless branches flailing the air while the evergreens bent almost double and cracked menacingly.

By the time they reached the churchyard, it was getting dark. They paused for a moment under the lych-gate, and listened to the wind whistling round and round the gravestones. Suddenly, from the far end of the churchyard, they saw a light flash. On, off, it went. On. Off. On. Off.

'What's that?' said Asa.

Tom shrugged. 'Only one way to find out,' he said, and set off towards the flashing light.

As they got closer, Tom began to feel anxious. His stomach knotted and his heart began to pound. He felt that he was being drawn onwards – whether he liked it or not. The last time this had happened, he had found himself in front of storeroom number nine. What, he wondered nervously, were he and Asa about to discover now?

Closer still, and they saw the light was coming from beneath an ancient beech tree silhouetted against the slate-grey sky. Unlike the others, the tree hadn't shed all its leaves, though those that remained were dead. And, as the wind set the tree bowing, up and down, they rustled like a thousand brown paper bags.

'It isn't a light at all,' said Asa suddenly.

Tom stopped and looked. His friend was right. When the beech tree reached up, something polished and shiny beneath it mirrored the fading daylight; when it bowed down again, a dark shadow blotted out the reflection. Up. Down. On. Off. Asa went a couple of steps further on.

'It's just a gravestone,' he said.

Tom nodded dully. He'd already guessed as much. 'Whose?' he said.

From Asa's sharp intake of breath, Tom knew the answer.

'Silas Grimsby's,' they announced as one.

While most of the graves in the churchyard were marked with simple stone crosses, Silas Grimsby's headstone was an elaborate affair. Carved from a piece of solid marble, it was shaped like a scroll. Two trumpeting angels decorated the top. What was more, the engraving had been done to last. Even in the half light, more than a century after they had been cut, the words looked as if they had only just been chiselled into the stone. Both Tom and Asa shuddered as they read the ominous message.

Here lieth the body of Silas Grimsby.
Or most thereof . . .

Beneath this were three dates:

Born: 2nd February, 1854 – Died: 15th
& 22nd March, 1869

And beneath this, an inscription that chilled both boys to the marrow.

'I shall not rest until I am whole
And I curse all those who thwart this
goal.'

Behind them, the chapel bell chimed the hour. Tom trembled.

'Four o'clock,' he said. 'Eight hours before the hand appears again.'

Asa smiled weakly. 'I can hardly wait,' he said.

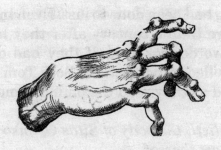

11

RATTLING BONES

Shortly after lights out, Tom had heard the sounds of Asa stirring. The moment he had been dreading had finally arrived. It was time to return to Storeroom 9.

'Shake a leg,' he heard Asa whispering urgently. 'We've got to get there and back before the Baxters do their rounds.'

'Coming,' said Tom. He pushed the bedclothes back, climbed out of his warm bed and slipped his dressing-gown and slippers on. They felt cold and clammy. 'And you're sure Eva doesn't want to come,' he said.

'Sure,' said Asa. 'I told you. She said, and I quote "white horses wouldn't drag me there".'

'*White* horses?' Tom said and laughed. 'I thought it was *wild* horses.'

'That's what she said,' Asa replied. 'Perhaps it's what they say in Swiss.'

'German,' said Tom.

'I thought . . .'

'The Swiss speak German,' said Tom. 'Well, most of them. Some speak French, or Italian – and there's some other language as well . . . But most of them speak German. Swiss German.'

'Whatever,' said Asa. 'She's not coming.'

Lucky her, Tom thought, as he followed Asa across the dormitory and out into the corridor.

The desolate howl of the wind outside echoed round the building as Asa and Tom made their way cautiously down the stairs to the floor below. It was as though Styles Grange was breathing. In and out. In and out. And as it breathed, so it creaked, and squeaked, and rattled, and moaned. Each and every noise set the two boys glancing round nervously. They knew they were doing something absolutely forbidden. They knew what would happen if they were caught. Each creak and squeak, every rattle and moan seemed to be announcing the arrival of the dreaded Miss Bennett.

Only when they finally reached Storeroom 9 did Asa dare to switch on his torch. He shone the light at the keyhole. Tom, who had been clutching the key so tightly it had made deep indentations on his finger and thumb, now pushed it into the lock. Scarcely daring to breathe, he turned the key. There was a soft click as the mechanism was released. Asa tried the handle – and the door swung open.

Now they were there, there was no turning back. Asa and Tom went inside the room. Tom shut the door behind him. 'What now?' he said.

Asa shone the torch around the small dusty room. Like the others Tom had seen, this too was full of various bits and pieces from the school. Whereas Storerooms 2, 5 and 8 had been home to books, sports gear and theatrical props, Storeroom 9 had been used to store various bits of paraphernalia from the science laboratories.

There were shelves full of retorts and pipettes, tripods, mats and Bunsen burners. There were piles of magazines and heaps of ancient text books. As Asa shone the torch upwards, the beam of light glinted on row upon row of glass jars. Some were empty. Some had been filled, to various levels, with liquids of various colour. Some were stoppered; some had screw-tops.

One jar was filled with bulls' eyes. Real ones. Floating in a clear solution, they were staring round in all directions. Another was full of pickled frogs; another contained tiny internal organs – kidneys, livers, hearts. While in the corner, up high, was a large jar with something large and pink inside it – something which glistened sickeningly in the torchlight.

Tom swallowed queasily. His forehead was wet with sweat. It was like being in a witch's stock-room, jam-packed full with all the ingredients for every possible wicked spell.

It was Asa who brought him back down to earth. The contents of the various jars, he explained, would have been used in classroom experiments. 'You know,' he said, wrinkling up his nose. 'Dissection!'

Tom nodded. Of course, that was it. The various animals – and parts of animals – belonged to a time when biology meant getting blood on your hands; a time when boys were not allowed to be so squeamish. Suddenly, something occurred to him. Something that sent shivers shooting up and down his spine.

'You don't think . . .' he began.

'What?' said Asa.

'You don't think the hand is . . . is . . .' He waved towards the shelves of bottled bodies and body parts. 'Is up there somewhere,' he said.

Asa said nothing. The same thought had already occurred to him. After all, it made sense. They knew from the prospectus that the severed hand had gone missing; they knew from the graveyard that the spirit of Silas Grimsby would not rest until his body was whole again. Why else would the hand have led them here?

'Well?' said Tom impatiently.

Asa sighed. 'There's only one way to find out,' he said at last.

Tom groaned. The thought of rummaging through the jars for the one that contained the severed hand filled him with dread. At first, he thought he was going to escape the ordeal. Since the shelves were so high up, they would need something to stand on. Sadly, Asa found exactly what they needed at the end of the room. There, leaning up against a heavy oak wardrobe, was a step-ladder.

'We'll take it in turns,' said Asa, as he crossed the room. 'I'll look first, but then it's your go.' He picked up the steps and carried them to the shelves. 'OK?' he said.

Tom made no reply.

'OK?' Asa repeated. He looked up and shone the torch at Tom. He saw the look of absolute terror in his face. 'Wh . . . wh . . . what's the matter?' he said.

He spun round to where Tom's petrified gaze was fixed. The door of the wardrobe continued to swing open. It creaked eerily. Wider and wider it swung as if something – or someone – inside was pushing it.

Asa shone the torch into the widening gap. As he did so, the beam of light struck something white.

The door gave an abrupt lurch, and opened completely. And there, hanging from the clothes rail, by a hook which had been screwed into its skull, was a skeleton.

Asa gasped and clamped his hand over his mouth; Tom bit into one of his fingers. Both of them tried desperately not to do what they so wanted to do – to scream aloud at the tops of their voices.

The skeleton grinned back at them malevolently. The empty black sockets of its eyes glared. As the door swung back to its furthest extent, the whole wardrobe shook. And the skeleton – the grinning, glaring bag of bones – rattled and jigged in a weird and sinister dance.

This was more than either boy could bear. Asa dropped the torch; there was the sound of splintering glass and the light went out. Tom, whose entire body was shaking like the skeleton itself, cried out as the storeroom was plunged into darkness.

He couldn't stand it there a moment longer. Turning towards the door, he fumbled round desperately for the handle.

'Got to get out of here,' he panted. 'We've got to escape!'

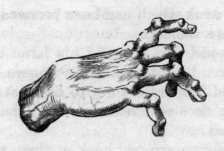

12

SPILT BLOOD

It was only later, when their hearts had finally stopped hammering, that Asa and Tom were able to look rationally at what had happened. The step-ladder had been keeping the wardrobe door shut. When it was removed, the door had swung open. That was all. And the skeleton? It was just one more odd piece of equipment from the biology lab.

Simple though the explanation was, the incident had frightened both boys. As they pulled their quilts up high over their shoulders and wished each other goodnight, they both prayed that their sleep would not be disturbed by nightmares of dancing skeletons.

Tom cuddled Mister Bear close to his chest,

and closed his eyes. Despite, or perhaps because of all the terrifying excitement of the day, he fell asleep at once.

The next minute – at least, that was what it felt like – Tom was roughly awoken. Something was tugging at his quilt and scraping at his shoulder. The sound of the bell echoed dolefully round the room.

Tom blinked his eyes open and twisted round. It was the hand. Again!

'What now?' he murmured, more with impatience than fear. Even the most ghoulish of objects lose their shock value by the third appearance.

As if in response, the hand seized his pyjama jacket behind the neck, yanked Tom out of bed and – crash – on to the floor. Then, with a strength that horrified him, it tugged Tom back to his feet and dragged him towards the door.

Now Tom *was* frightened. He was petrified!

'Help!' he cried out. 'Asa . . . Wake up! ASA!'

Asa opened his eyes to see Tom disappearing out through the dormitory door. It struck him as odd that his friend's feet hardly seemed to be touching the ground. When the bell rang for a fifth time, he realized why it was happening.

'Hang on,' he bellowed. 'I'm coming!'

As he raced past the Baxters' room, he heard the sound of snoring. In stereo. Asa paused, wondering whether he should wake them up. As

111

the bell tolled for the sixth time, he decided against it. There simply wasn't time.

At the top of the stairs, Asa skidded to a halt and peered down over the banisters. Tom was already down on the second floor – and being dragged still further by the hand. Asa flew down the stairs, two at a time and skidding round on the balls of his feet at every landing. At the first floor, he saw Tom disappearing inside a room half-way along the corridor.

'The library!' he panted.

Without pausing to wonder what the hand might want with him there, Asa hurtled along the passageway after them, and slipped in through the door just as it was swinging shut. The bell tolled again. Asa stopped running – but there was no time to catch his breath.

Tom was standing in the middle of the room. He was looking up. Asa followed his gaze, and there it was – scuttling along the very top of the bookcase in a cloud of dust. The hand.

Suddenly it stopped and disappeared into the dark shadows. The next moment it returned. It was clutching a book, which it tossed down on to the floor. It landed at Tom's feet.

The bell chimed for the twelfth time. The hand flew towards the leaded window-diamonds – and was gone.

Tom crouched down and picked the book up. It was dark in the library, but he was just able to make out the title. *'The Hauntings of Styles Grange,'* he read.

'That's it!' said Asa excitedly. 'That was the book Dr Buchanan showed us. It's by somebody Pritchard . . .'

'Eric,' said Tom.

'Eric Pritchard,' Asa nodded. 'I remember now. Apparently, he used to teach here – but before I came.' He looked down at the book. 'I hope there's something interesting in it,' he said, and laughed nervously. 'The hand seems to think there is.'

Tom nodded. 'The hand's not the only one,' he said grimly. 'Why would it be tucked away on the top shelf – unless someone was trying to hide it? Let's go and find out why.'

Unable to go back to sleep without first discovering why the book was so important, Asa and Tom sat huddled together on Asa's bed, poring over the pages by the light of Tom's torch – since Asa's was still lying, broken, on the storeroom floor. As they read through the chapters, they marked certain passages lightly with a pencil; passages which shed further light on the mysterious hand.

For a start, they discovered the awful truth of what really happened on that fateful night of the fifteenth of March, 1869. For the most part, the details agreed with the description in the prospectus, yet there was more – much more – about the role in the affair of the owner of the manor-house.

Although Wolfgang Geisselhardt had indeed taken on young Silas when his mother had died, he was neither a soft nor a sentimental man. Indeed, it was his hard – sometimes brutal – character that had helped create his wealth. No, the reasons he had employed Silas Grimsby were these: he knew the boy was honest, and he knew he would work hard. Nothing else had influenced his decision.

So it was that when Silas' hand became ensnared in the ropes, Geisselhardt hadn't cared a jot about the welfare of the boy. It was *he* who refused to allow the ropes to be cut since he would not even consider any course of action which might have endangered the costly bell. Instead, when all else had failed, he seized hold of the hand and, using his own hunting knife, severed it at the wrist himself.

'But . . . Silas must have known,' said Asa.

'I know,' Tom said, and shuddered. 'And then to *lose* the hand! Does it say what happened to it?'

Asa shone the torch back down on the text. *And the hand, which fell away into the darkness, was never seen again* they read, and were none the wiser.

Continuing on to the next pages, they discovered that the phantom hand had already made three sets of appearances that century. The first was in the storms of 1903. Apparently sensing imminent danger to the bell, the hand had somehow brought firemen to the scene, minutes before the church tower had been struck by lightning. Since they were already there, the firemen had managed to douse the flames before the fire caused any major damage.

The second appearance occurred during the war. It was 1944 and the manor-house – by now a school – was evacuated. The boys' places had been taken by soldiers. It was one of them who was alerted by the hand to an approaching enemy bomber. He spun his ack-ack gun round and shot the plane down, seconds before it could drop its bombs on the buildings below. It crashed in the woods half a mile away and exploded into flame.

Both Asa and Tom already knew about the hand's next appearance – or rather, appearances. That had been back in 1976, when the proposed by-pass had, for a third time, threatened the bell. What they didn't know, but what they now read, was that Jake Armitage – the boy who had first seen the hand – had been killed.

Tom swallowed. 'Someone died,' he said. 'Someone actually died.'

Apparently, he was found lying on the hard tiles at the bottom of the chapel tower. The post-mortem reported that he must have fallen at least twenty metres. No-one ever discovered what he had been doing up there that night, crawling around in the rafters.

'But why didn't Mr Baxter tell us?' said Asa.

'Perhaps he didn't want to frighten us,' said Tom, shaking his head nervously.

Suddenly, the whole situation had changed. Before, although terrifying, neither Tom nor Asa had thought the hand could do them real harm. Now they knew they were wrong.

The hand was playing a deadly game. Understanding the rules of that game had become, for the two boys, a matter of life and death.

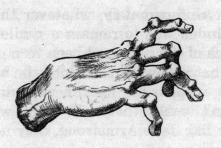

13

THE PROFESSOR'S WARNING

At breakfast the following morning, Asa and Tom were both bleary eyed and tired. It had been almost half past three when they had finally climbed back into their beds and rolled over on to their sides. Their bodies were exhausted, yet even then their heads had continued to spin with all the awful facts and figures they had uncovered.

They now knew almost all there was to know – and yet, one key question remained unanswered. Why had the hand chosen to reappear now?

For a while, they thought they had found the answer in Eric Pritchard's book. *'The conclusion to be drawn from all of this is as follows . . .'* they had read. Unfortunately, whatever the writer *had* concluded was to remain a riddle, for the final pages of the book had been torn out. Tom guessed that whoever had hidden the book, had also been responsible for the vandalism. But that didn't really help. If they were not to end up like Jake Armstrong, they needed to discover what the hand was actually trying to achieve.

It was Eva who came up with the obvious solution. Having listened to the two boys' excited recounting of events – the prospectus, the hand, the book with its missing conclusion, the dead boy – she laid her spoon down thoughtfully.

'I remember Mr Pritchard,' she said slowly. 'He gave an assembly once – don't *you* remember him, Asa?'

Asa nodded doubtfully.

'Typical,' Eva sniffed. 'Important is, that Dr Buchanan introduced him as a local historian – a *local* historian. He lives in the village. I think you'll find his address at the back of the book. All we've got to do is go and see him – so long as we can all sneak out without being noticed.'

Tom grinned. 'We?' he said.

'Pardon?'

'You said, "all *we've* got to do . . ." Are you going to come with us?'

'Naturally,' said Eva. 'If what you have said is true, we are *all* in danger. Me included! Anyway,

118

you could do with my help, I think.'

'We were getting along just fine, thank you very much,' said Asa hotly.

Eva smiled. 'You forgot about Eric Pritchard,' she said, as she pushed back her chair. 'Who can tell what else you might have forgotten?'

Asa bit into his lip angrily. 'Right, then,' he said finally. 'Shall we go?'

To his surprise, Eva burst out laughing. 'You see what I mean,' she said.

'What?' said Asa. 'WHAT?'

'We've got Morning Meeting first,' said Tom quietly.

As Eva disappeared up to her room, Asa turned to Tom and exploded. 'Well, of all the . . .! Blimey! She can be so smug! After all we've been through, I . . . I . . .'

Tom smiled. He hadn't seen his friend this angry before. 'We're in a fix,' he said. 'Three heads are bound to be better than two!'

Eva, it turned out, was right on both counts. Eric Pritchard's address *was* at the back of the book – his next project concerned the mysterious goings-on at a certain Witten Priory, and any reader of *The Hauntings of Styles Grange* with information on the priory was encouraged to write to him direct. What was more, the address was indeed local.

As the chapel bell tolled the half-hour far away

behind them, Eva, Asa and Tom were standing on Eric Pritchard's doorstep waiting for the door to be answered.

'Do you think I should try again?' said Asa.

'Leave it a bit longer,' said Tom. 'If . . .'

At that moment, the door swung open.

'Yes?' said a woman. She was tall and elegant, with green eyes and a stylish, greying bob. 'Can I help you?' she said.

'We are sorry to bother you,' said Eva, 'but does a Mr Eric Pritchard still live here. We . . .'

'*Professor* Pritchard, yes,' she said.

'We have been reading one of his books but, unfortunately, the end has been torn . . .'

Suddenly a voice resounded from deep inside the house. 'Who is it, my dear?'

The woman turned. 'Three children,' she said. 'They have some questions about your book.'

'My book!' the voice exclaimed. 'Oh, how wonderful.' The children heard the sound of footsteps hurrying down the stairs. The next instant, the door flew wide open, and they were confronted by a tall, white-haired man beaming down at them. 'Come in, come in,' he said. 'We shall go to my study . . . Martha,' he said, turning to his wife. 'Would you be an angel and see to some refreshments. Some buns, perhaps . . .' he added vaguely.

Mrs Pritchard smiled. 'I'll see what I can do,' she said.

'Champion!' Professor Pritchard said, and clapped his hands together. 'Right, this way.'

Overwhelmed, the children followed the professor into his study. When they had arrived at Knapp Cottage, they hadn't known what to expect. Eva had suggested they simply ask whether he had a spare copy of the book for sale. Certainly they hadn't imagined that he would be so friendly and enthusiastic about their enquiries.

'Vandals! Barbarians! Philistines!' he roared, when he saw the damage that had been done to the school copy of his book. 'Who on earth would do such a thing?' And he cradled the book to his chest as if it were an injured child.

'So, what *was* your conclusion?' asked Tom.

Professor Pritchard looked up. 'My conclusion,' he repeated. 'It was wide-ranging but not, I think far-fetched. I suggested, because of the evidence, that there was a definite link between the bell and the hand. It was, after all, *because* of the bell, that the hand became separated from the rest of the body. I suggested that when the bell felt itself to be in danger, it would rouse the spirit of the hand to come to its aid . . .'

'But, Professor Pritchard,' said Eva, 'how can a bell *feel* anything?'

The man shook his head. 'A good question,' he said. 'And one which, when I was writing the book, remained unresolved. However, I recently received an interesting letter concerning the foundry works where the bell was manufactured.'

'The Josiah Boothroyd Works,' said Tom, remembering the name he'd seen in the prospectus.

'Quite right,' said the professor. 'Now the bell, you will recall, was made in 1868. The following year, the entire works was burned to the ground. At first it was thought to be an accident. Only later was it established that the fire had been started deliberately. What was more, someone – a woman – died in the fire.' He paused. 'I haven't managed to establish *exactly* what she was doing there, but the newspapers at the time suggested that it was some kind of magic ritual which had gone fatally wrong.'

'You mean she was a *witch*?' said Tom.

Professor Pritchard shook his head. 'I don't think so,' he said. 'At least, not in the conventional sense. Certainly I do not believe that the bell is in any way evil. In fact, rather the opposite. The arcane rituals used would have instilled in it the power of protection, not destruction.'

'*Old* magic rather than *black* magic,' said Eva.

'Precisely,' said the professor. 'Though, of course, we shall never know for sure. Whatever secrets the Works might have concealed were all destroyed in the fire. However,' he added, and breathed in sharply, 'we must ask ourselves this. If magic – any kind of magic – *was* involved in the making of the bell, then who is to say what powers it might now possess?'

The three children fell silent. They had already realized that something linked the bell and the hand – after all, the hand only appeared when the bell was tolling midnight. What they hadn't imagined, was that the bell might, in some way, be influencing the increasingly menacing behaviour of the hand.

It was Eva who finally broke the silence. 'You said that the hand acts to protect the bell,' she said. Professor Pritchard nodded. 'So what happens if it fails?' she asked. 'What would the hand do then?'

The professor looked down, and shook his head. 'That poor boy,' he said. 'Jake Armitage. I used to teach him Latin. It was his death that inspired me to write the book . . .'

He raised his head and looked at the three children in turn. 'What would the hand of Silas Grimsby do if anything happened to the bell?' he said. 'I believe it would destroy Styles Grange completely.'

'But how?' said Eva. 'What could a hand . . ?'

'Since it reappeared,' the professor interrupted, 'have any unexplained problems arisen in the school?'

'There's the boiler,' said Tom.

123

'And the cool-room,' said Asa, shuddering just at the thought of the place.

'And there was a power cut the other night,' said Tom.

'You see! You see!' the professor blustered. 'And don't try and tell me it's all just a coincidence. How easy it would be for the wiring system to short-circuit, for the school to burn down . . .' His eyes glazed over. *'If any harm should befall the bell, then Heaven help us all,'* he whispered.

At that moment, the door burst open. Eva, Asa and Tom all jumped. The professor looked up.

'Ah, Martha,' he said. 'Wonderful.' He jumped up, took the laden tray and placed it on his desk. 'Coffee all round, is it?' he said. 'Milk?'

The children nodded.

'Professor Pritchard,' said Asa. 'What you just said . . .'

'What *did* I just say?' he asked, sounding somewhat surprised.

'If any harm should be . . . be . . .'

'. . . befall the bell; yes, yes.'

'Well, who said that?'

'Oh, I understand,' he said. 'Yes, silly of me – I should have mentioned it before. Much of my information came from the diaries of Wolfgang Geisselhardt.'

'The bloke who built Styles Grange in the first place,' said Asa.

'Quite so,' said the professor. 'He was a most remarkable man in many ways. Originally an entrepreneur from Zürich, he was a millionaire by the time he was thirty. A millionaire! In those days! Anyway, apart from his many other talents, he was also a keen diarist. The problem is, however . . .' He stood up and retrieved a bulging folder from the top shelf. 'The problem is,' he said again, 'some of the entries are written in code – particularly towards the end. And I'm afraid to say it is a code which has me utterly baffled.'

He handed the folder to Tom. 'Here,' he said. 'Take it. Perhaps you'll succeed where I failed.'

Tom peeked in. It contained two thick diaries and a sheaf of documents. 'Are you sure?' he said.

'Oh, yes,' said Professor Pritchard darkly. 'If the situation is as dangerous as I believe it is, then you are going to need all the help you can get. You must promise me though that you'll be careful. Too much blood has already been spilt at Styles Grange.'

14

DEAD END

The diaries made interesting reading. Up in Eva's dormitory, she read one, while Asa and Tom looked at the other. All three of them skimmed through the entries, piping up with any titbits that they thought interesting. As for the sections written in code, however, they drew a blank.

'It looks like a transpositional code,' said Tom.

'Does it now?' said Asa, winking at Eva.

'Yeah, you know,' said Tom. 'Where you write out the alphabet, and then choose one of the letters – E for instance, to be A, and alter all the letters in the same way. So B becomes F, C becomes G, D becomes H and so on.'

The trouble was, no matter which letter they

chose as their starting point, the decoded message was still in gobbledygook.

'Hopeless,' Asa muttered irritably, as his tenth attempt proved to be as incomprehensible as the rest. 'I'm going down for lunch!'

The afternoon proved to be just as frustrating. Dividing up the letters between them, they continued to try to decode sentences from the diaries, but still with no success.

At three o'clock, Asa and Tom finally kept their appointment in the gym. After nearly an hour of sparring – with Asa teaching Tom the rudiments of the sport – the two boys were both short of breath and sweating. Tom turned his attention, instead, to the punch-bag.

He soon discovered how good it felt pummelling the soft, heavy bag. As his blows grew more and more frenzied, the anger, fear and frustration that had been building up inside him began slowly to disappear.

After a shower, the boys split up. Asa returned to the diaries; Tom went to the Junior Common Room, where Eva was waiting for him. That morning, Miss Bennett had asked the children to tidy everything away and sort out the cupboards. They hadn't been looking forward to it, but in the event it didn't take long and, when they had finished, they settled down for a game of chess. When the gong sounded for dinner, Tom was down to four pieces. Two moves later, it was all over. Eva had trapped his king with her queen and bishop. Checkmate.

Tom flicked his king over on to its side and stared down at the three solitary pawns remaining, abandoned, on the board. 'I hope it's not an omen,' he said quietly.

Eva sighed. 'It is not knowing what will happen next that is so worrying,' she said. 'I wonder if Asa has had any luck with the code yet.'

'I hope so,' said Tom grimly. 'I hope so.'

Unfortunately, Asa had not managed to solve the code system. And, though all three of them spent the whole evening trying all kinds of variations on the 'transpositional' theory, not once did they come up with a sentence that looked remotely like a language. By the time lights-out arrived, they knew they had failed.

Asa – it was true – had made one discovery. In the prospectus, he had found a photograph of the Colts Rugby XV. In the front row, third from the right, was a dark-haired boy with a big, cheeky grin. It was Jake Armitage, unaware of the fate which lay in store for him. The sight of the boy's innocently happy face only made the children feel all the worse.

If Wolfgang Geisselhardt *had* included some vital clue in his diaries about Silas Grimsby's hand, they had not found it. As a result, the hand was bound to reappear that night. And when they climbed into their beds, each of them was aware that this was not so much the end of the day, as the beginning of the night – a night they would all have given anything to avoid.

Tom tossed and turned under his quilt. His brain spun and sleep would not come. Whenever he closed his eyes, two images flashed before him. One, the hand, at the moment the knife severed it at the wrist. Two, the smiling face of Jake Armitage – the boy who would subsequently end up lying on the floor of the chapel tower with blood trickling from his mouth.

Finally, Tom could stand it no more. He sat up, climbed out of bed and went to the window. The bright moon was appearing and disappearing behind a succession of small fluffy clouds that bounded across the sky like sheep. Without thinking, Tom tried to let in some fresh air – he'd forgotten that the windows were all bolted shut.

The noise woke Asa. 'What are you doing?' he asked drowsily.

'I can't sleep,' said Tom.

'No,' said Asa, and yawned. 'Neither can I.'

Tom smiled. He didn't mention that his friend clearly *had* been asleep. Tom stared down the hill at the pond; now silver, now black. 'I wish we weren't locked in,' he said. 'Especially after what the professor said about fires.'

'There is a way out,' said Asa, sitting up. He

grinned. 'Midnight feasts are even better outside,' he said.

'Where is it?' said Tom.

'The way out?' said Asa. 'On that corridor leading to the annexe. There's always a key in it.' He looked at Tom. 'Why?' he said. 'Thinking of going for a walk?'

Tom nodded. 'It's this place,' he said. 'The hand . . . the bell . . .'

As he spoke, the bell in question started to chime. Asa looked hurriedly at his watch. 'Phew!' he said. 'Only eleven o'clock.'

Tom smiled weakly. 'I just want to go home,' he sighed, and looked back out of the window.

From the heaving of his shoulders, Asa could see that his friend was crying. He didn't know what to say. Of course, the appearances of the hand weren't helping, but he knew that they were not the real cause of Tom's unhappiness. He was a *sad*: he wanted to be with his parents.

Asa had seen it all before. Even though he had never felt the pangs of separation himself, he recognized homesickness in others. And he envied it, he envied it so much. He envied Tom, who was missing the warmth and tenderness of his family; he envied Eva, who was missing the company of her brother and father; he envied everyone who missed someone – for Asa did not miss anyone.

As he continued to watch his friend silently

weeping by the window, Asa felt the lack of love in his own life all the more strongly. Asa Martin might be a *glad* – relieved to have escaped the domestic mayhem of his home – but his schoolmates' homesickness made him more miserable than any of the *sads* could ever be.

'Go for that walk,' he said quietly. 'But make sure you're back here by twelve.'

'Otherwise I'll turn into a pumpkin?' said Tom.

'Just be here,' said Asa.

'I will,' said Tom. 'I promise.'

Ten minutes later, Tom was sitting on a tree stump down at the water's edge. Despite the tracksuit he had slipped over his pyjamas, and jacket he had put on over that, he was still cold. The wind – gathering speed with every passing minute – was coming from the north-east. It made his eyes water; it made his ears throb.

In his left hand, Tom was holding a stick; in his right hand, the Swiss Army knife. He had already whittled one end into a sharp point. As he continued to slice at the stick, shavings, as fine as petals, were whipped away by the wind.

'They love me,' Tom murmured. 'They love me not. They love me. They . . .' The blade caught for a second on a tiny knot. Tom eased the knife through the harder wood, the shaving broke free and flew off after the rest. '. . . love me not.'

When he first heard the rustling in the trees,

Tom assumed, without giving it too much thought, that it must be an animal. A fox, perhaps. Or a badger. When a twig cracked, however, he became alarmed.

'That's a person,' he whispered to himself. He leapt to his feet and peered into the shadows of the trees. 'Who's there?' he hissed. 'Asa, if that's you . . .'

'It isn't Asa,' came a voice. 'It's me.'

'Eva!' said Tom. 'You scared me half to death. What on earth are you doing down here at this time of night?'

'I could ask you the same thing,' said Eva. She sighed. 'But I suppose the answer would be the same. I come here to think about my family. My brother, my father – my Oma . . .'

'*Oma?*' said Tom.

'Grandmother,' said Eva. 'My mother's mother. Daddy won't talk about my mother. Oma is my only link . . .' She shook her head. 'I was three-and-a-half when she died,' she said. 'Three-and-a-half! And do you know what? I cannot remember a single day with her. *Keinen einzigen Tag.*' She took a deep breath and looked at Tom. 'What is it you say? Absence makes the heart grow fonder?'

Tom nodded.

'Well, it's wrong,' said Eva bitterly. 'Completely wrong. Absence makes the heart forget.'

132

'Oh, Eva,' said Tom. He felt awkward, clumsy; he didn't know what to do. Everything told him to give the girl a hug. But he didn't want to comfort her. That was her father's job, not his. Just as it was his parents' job to comfort him. But they can't, can they? he thought angrily. Because they aren't here!

In the end, it was Eva who made the decision. She flung open her arms and wrapped them around Tom. He, in turn, hugged her back. And there they stood, at the water's edge, with the moon coming and going behind the clouds. Tom and Eva; two lonely children clutching to one another for a little bit of the warmth they both missed so much.

Suddenly, the sound of the chapel bell cut through the night air. Tom pulled away.

'Midnight!' he cried. 'I said I'd be back by now. I promised.'

Tom had realized that Asa – big, brave, boxing Asa – was terrified of confronting the hand alone. Now it was too late for him to do anything about it.

The next instant, Eva screamed. Tom looked up in alarm. As he saw the tiny object speeding towards them from out of the distance, he knew that Asa had nothing to fear that night. The hand would not be paying any visits to the dormitory.

As it got closer, Tom saw that the hand was

flying with its index and middle finger extended. Closer still, and he watched the fingers parting to form a V shape. And still it kept coming.

All at once, it occurred to Tom where it was aiming. At him – or, to be more precise, at his eyes. Unable to move, he stared in horror as the razor-sharp nails of the two splayed fingers hurtled towards his eyeballs. 'NO!' he screamed, and screwed his eyes tightly shut.

The next moment, the hand struck.

But not at his eyes, nor at any other part of his body. Instead, as Tom remained frozen to the spot, too frightened to look, he felt the Swiss Army knife being plucked from his grasp.

'Not the knife!' Tom roared, furious that the hand should dare to take something so precious to him. He looked round him angrily. The hand had not gone far. It was hovering some three or four metres away. 'Give it back!' Tom shouted, and lunged forward. The hand darted back and away. 'Come here!' Tom yelled. 'Give me back my kn—'

The word caught in his throat as he realized what he was saying. And, as the hand deftly pulled out the larger of the two blades and waved it menacingly in the air, Tom backed off. 'Not like that,' he said, suddenly alarmed. 'I didn't mean . . .'

But it was too late. Once again, the hand was flying towards him; the open blade glinted in the

moonlight. 'Gotta run,' Tom said. 'Gotta hide.'
But the hand was too fast. Before Tom had even
turned away, it was upon him.

Revenge, he thought. That's what the hand's
after. Revenge. Pure and simple. An eye for an
eye, a tooth for a tooth – and a hand for a hand.

Just then, the knife disappeared from view.
Tom spun round in terror. Where was it? Where
had it gone? He soon found out.

Something cold and hard was touching his
skin. He looked down to see the severed hand
drawing the knife sharply across his own wrist.
He screamed. Eva ran towards him.

'Tom!' she cried. 'Are you all right?'

Tom stared at his wrist. There was a dull red
line across the skin. He wiggled his fingers
around, and nodded.

'Yes,' he said. 'It was . . . it was the back of the
blade. Oh, Eva, I thought . . .'

'It's just trying to tell us what happened,' said
Eva. 'Don't you see? Bit by bit, it's giving us the
events – in the only way it can.'

'I know,' said Tom quietly. But the feel of the
cold steel against his skin had frightened him.
He felt so vulnerable.

Yet the hand had not cut him. Tom knew he
had to hold on to this fact. It did not mean them
harm – at least not yet.

'It wants us to follow it,' said Eva.

Tom looked up. Suspended in mid-air, the

hand was beckoning impatiently. Suddenly, overcome with weariness – yet knowing he could not ignore the hand's command – Tom set off with Eva, up the hill after it.

As they ran, so the bell continued to chime. *Six. Seven. Eight.* Both Tom and Eva knew that the hand could have flown faster if it wanted. It could have escaped them in the twinkling of an eye. But it didn't. It hovered just out of reach as the three of them hurried back to Styles Grange. Once, when Tom stopped running altogether, the hand paused too and waved the knife about in the air. Like a donkey following a carrot, Tom found the strength to take him a few steps further.

And the bell tolled. *Nine. Ten.* It was almost time for the hand to disappear once more. What if they hadn't reached their destination by then? What if the hand was unable to show them whatever it was it had found?

As the bell chimed for the eleventh time, the hand halted abruptly in mid-air. It seemed to be trying to decide what to do. *Twelve.* All at once, the hand flicked forward and sent the knife flying through the air.

Tom didn't notice the flutter of fingers as the hand waved them goodbye. Nor did he see it disappear. He was watching his knife as it spun, over and over, far away into the distance. Trying

136

hard not to blink – not to take his eyes away from it for even a moment – he raced on after it.

As the knife reached the top of its arc and began falling back down towards the ground, Tom increased his speed until he was sprinting as fast as he could. He would not lose the knife. He simply would not!

He heard Eva panting behind him. 'It's going to hit the window!' she gasped.

Tom stopped and watched in horror as the knife continued its spinning descent. If it smashed the glass they were going to be in *real* trouble. The next moment, Tom sighed with relief. The knife had landed in the earth of the bare flower-bed in front of the window, and buried itself up to the red plastic hilt.

He went to dash forwards – only to be seized by the arm. 'Watch out,' Eva warned him urgently. 'There's a light on.'

Tom looked up. She was right. What was more, as he stared at the orange glow streaming through the glass, he realized whose room it was: Miss Bennett's.

'What's she doing in her office so late?' said Tom.

Eva shrugged. 'Something the hand wanted us to see,' she said.

Bent low, he and Eva tiptoed towards the window and crouched down below the sill. Tom pulled the blade from the earth, wiped it on his tracksuit bottoms and slipped the knife into his pocket. Above him he could hear the faint murmur of voices – or rather, a voice.

'She's talking to herself,' said Eva.

'I knew she was crazy,' said Tom.

Cautiously, the two children pulled themselves up and peered into the room. They saw Miss Bennett striding back and forwards across the floor. She *was* talking – but not because she had gone mad. There was a tape-machine on the desk, recording every word of the letter she was composing.

She spoke of the school's 'temporary cash-flow problem', she spoke of 'ill-advised forays into the stock market', she spoke about 'an imminent windfall' and pleaded that her 'personal credit be extended for a few days more'. To most children, the words would have meant nothing – but to Tom, the son of a banker, the situation was crystal clear.

Miss Bennett was in deep financial trouble. She had invested the school's money badly, and now the bank was demanding that she repay her debts in full. But what about the 'windfall'? he wondered. And how much were they actually talking about?

And then Tom remembered. He turned to Eva. '"When I say a million, I *mean* a million",' he

138

whispered. 'That was what she said.' And he told her about the telephone conversation he and his parents had overheard that first afternoon at Styles Grange. 'A million pounds,' he said. 'But where from?'

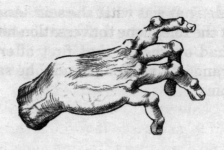

15

A DANGEROUS
CONCLUSION

'And you're sure that the hand led you there?'
Asa said.

'Yes,' said Tom.

'It couldn't just have been chance that the
knife landed where it did?' he persisted.

'No,' said Tom, shaking his head. 'I'm positive
we were meant to overhear what she was saying. The hand grabbed the knife, we chased after
it – and when the time ran out, it threw the knife
to exactly the right spot. It *can't* have been
chance.'

Asa turned his attention back to his breakfast.
He sliced off a soldier of toast and dunked it into

his boiled egg. 'What I still don't understand,' he said, looking up, 'is why the hand doesn't just tell us direct.'

'How could it?' said Tom. 'It can hardly talk . . .'

'It can write,' Asa interrupted.

'Can it?' said Tom. 'I'm not so sure.'

'STORM 9,' said Asa. 'It wrote it three times.'

'Yes,' said Tom. 'But it meant something else, didn't it? I mean, anyone who could read would have *known* that there were missing letters. No,' he said frowning. 'I think the hand – or Silas Grimsby – or whatever, memorized what it saw without knowing what it was.'

Asa nodded. Certainly that would explain why the hand hadn't just left them a little note telling them what to do. He began munching the yolky toast. 'Fing iffthh,' he mumbled.

'Pardon?' said Tom.

Asa swallowed. 'The thing is,' he said, 'I'm still not sure what we should actually be trying to do. We know that the hand was amputated from a boy called Silas Grimsby, right?'

'Right,' said Tom.

'And we know that its spirit – or ghost – will not rest until the entire body is reunited, right?'

'Right.'

'But we also know that this spirit – or ghost – is only active when the bell is in danger, right?'

'Right,' said Tom for a third time.

141

'So what *are* we meant to be doing?' said Asa. 'Looking for the hand, or trying to save the bell from whatever it is that might or might not happen?'

Tom smiled down at his plate. It was something that he had been wondering himself, down by the pond. The bell or the hand? The hand or the bell? As far as he could see, there was only one conclusion. He looked up.

'Both,' he said quietly.

Asa sighed. 'I had the horrible feeling you were going to say that,' he said. 'So what *do* we do now?'

'I don't know what we *can* do,' said Tom. 'Except wait.'

At that moment, Eva burst into the dining hall, her face all pink and blotchy. 'WELL!' she exclaimed.

'What is it?' asked Tom.

'Miss Bennett!' she stormed. 'That . . . that . . .'

'Calm down,' Asa laughed. 'Begin at the beginning.'

Eva took a deep breath, and sat herself down opposite the two boys. 'I'd seen her earlier,' she explained. 'She came up to the dorm to ask if I could take a package to the village post office.'

Asa snorted. 'Yeah, she had us running errands for her, too.' He grinned. 'Perhaps we all ought to ask for pocket money.'

'Go on,' said Tom to Eva.

'Anyway, when I was dressed, I went down to her office, knocked on the door, and I *thought* she said "come in". So, in I went. She was on the phone, but with her back to me – looking out of the window. I stood there for a couple of minutes while she talked and talked. And then she turned round.

'When she saw me . . . I've never seen anyone so angry before. "How DARE you eavesdrop on my private conversation!" she said.'

'What *was* she saying?' asked Tom.

Eva shrugged. 'I don't know.'

'You must try and remember,' said Tom. 'It could be important.'

'Something . . . something about . . . Oh, I remember now,' she said. 'Like the Noah's Ark song. *The animals marching two by two . . .*' She screwed her face up, deep in thought. '. . . *two by two . . . in a . . .* That's right . . . *in a never-ending spiral . . .*'

'That's it!' Tom cried.

'What's it?' said Asa.

'All that stuff about the animals marching in twos,' said Tom impatiently. 'It's the chapel bell. Don't you remember?'

'The prospectus,' said Asa. "Course I do, but . . .'

'It's so obvious,' said Tom. 'I can't believe we've

143

been so dim! *That's* why she wrote all those letters. To antiques dealers.' He groaned. 'Antiques dealers who specialize in brass.'

'You mean . . .' said Asa.

Tom nodded. 'She's trying to sell the bell.' He looked at Eva. 'That explains the "windfall",' he said. 'A million-pound windfall!'

'To pay off her debts,' Eva added. 'You know what I think?' Tom and Asa shook their heads. 'I think she's been . . . been . . . ach! I don't know the word. When you take money from the place you are working . . .'

'Embezzling,' said Tom thoughtfully. 'You could be right, Eva. She did ask for her *personal* credit to be extended. And why else would she have reacted like she did when she realized that you'd overheard her?'

'That's *it*, then!' said Asa excitedly. 'Miss Bennett's had her hand in the school funds, and now she's trying to sell off the bell to cover her losses. We've cracked it.'

'Not quite,' said Tom.

'We *have!*' Asa insisted. 'Look, all we have to do now is let someone know what she's planning to do – maybe that professor. She gets stopped. The bell stays where it is. Danger over, and the hand disappears. End of story.'

'Yes,' said Tom. 'But . . .'

'*Yes, but*, what?' said Asa. 'It's all over.'

Tom shook his head. 'What about Silas Grimsby himself?' he asked. 'Surely we should still try to find the hand . . .'

'But why?' said Asa. 'If it's going to disappear anyway . . .'

'I don't know,' said Tom. 'To end its search once and for all.'

'It is not a happy spirit,' said Eva seriously.

'Oh, don't you start!' said Asa.

'Let me put it this way,' said Tom. *'I shall not rest until I am whole, and I curse – I CURSE – all those who thwart this goal.'*

Asa swallowed. He remembered the words on the gravestone well enough but, well, it was all nonsense, wasn't it? Yet, when Tom suggested a vote on whether to wait one more day before informing anyone about the bell, the decision was unanimous.

'So, where do we start looking?' said Asa. 'The thing disappeared over a hundred years ago. It was probably carried off somewhere by a dog, or . . . or a crow. It could be *anywhere* now. If it still exists at all. I mean, how long does it take a bone to turn to dust?'

'Oh, I'm sure it still exists,' said Tom.

'So am I,' Eva intervened. 'And I think I know where it might be.'

The two boys stared at her in amazement. 'Where?' they said in unison.

'Think about it,' he said. 'The hand appears when the bell is in danger. But why? I know there was all that stuff about old magic, but that doesn't explain *why* the hand comes to the bell's defence.'

'But . . .'

'Wait, Tom,' said Eva. 'I'm thinking aloud here. First there was the storm and the hand managed to bring fire fighters to the scene. Then there was the bomber plane which the hand succeeded in having destroyed. And then the plan for the by-pass . . .'

'We know all this,' Asa interrupted impatiently.

Eva nodded. 'I realize that,' she said patiently. 'But now imagine, just for a moment, that the hand isn't so much concerned with saving the bell, as saving itself. Now why might it have thought it was in danger from the lightning, or the bombs, or the bulldozers?'

'If it was . . . if it was in the same place as the bell,' said Tom slowly.

'*Genau!*' said Eva. 'Exactly. I don't think the hand was taken away. I don't think it ever left the tower at all. I think it's right there – probably only centimetres away from where it was cut off.'

Asa grinned. 'What are we waiting for?' he said, jumping up from his seat.

'There's just one other thing,' said Eva. 'I don't think I'm the first person to have worked this out.'

'What do you mean?' said Asa.

But Tom knew. He turned round to his friend. His face was deathly pale. 'Jake Armitage,' he said.

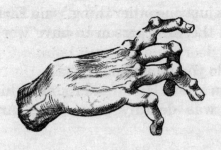

16

THE BELL TOWER

It was starting to rain as Tom, Eva and Asa made their way along the winding track which led to the chapel. The sky was ominously dark and the wind was getting up again. It was as if the same storm was circling the school, becoming stronger with each reappearance.

As the chapel tower loomed ahead of them, all three children stopped and stared with trepidation. The time on the clock was three minutes past nine. So much had already taken place within its four walls. What, exactly, were they about to let themselves in for now?

'Come on,' said Eva finally. 'We can't turn back now.'

Tom nodded. 'Eva's right,' he said, and

continued up the path towards the dark, carved entrance. 'Let's get this over with.'

As the door thudded shut behind them, they shuddered. The atmosphere inside the bell tower was overwhelming. It was cold, yet musty – and heavy with the awful events of the past.

Once the bell had been installed and the scaffolding removed, a series of ladders had been put in, to allow access to the loft. Originally, they had been made of stout wood. A hundred years of use, however, had left the banisters loose and the steps worn – in some places they were missing completely. It was up these rickety ladders that the three children nervously climbed, with Eva in front, Tom close behind her, and Asa bringing up the rear.

Up and up they went, one flight after the other. A dim light penetrated the gloom through narrow slits in the walls. The higher they climbed, the faster their hearts beat. Eva and Tom's imagination ran wild with all the possibilities of what might be awaiting them at the top. Asa, on the other hand, could think only of what lay below him: the fatally hard floor which, no matter how high he went, was still only a slip and a fall away.

'Don't look down,' he told himself miserably. 'Just don't look . . . woooooooaah!' Despite his own advice, Asa *had* looked down. The pattern of floor tiles swam crazily below him, telescoping in and out. He clutched at the wooden rungs desperately and tried to breathe more calmly. 'Easy does it,' he murmured to himself. 'Not far now.'

At that moment, Eva's head was just emerging through the small hole in the floor of the loft itself. Pigeons – alarmed at the appearance of the intruder – threw themselves into the air and flapped around noisily. Eva wrapped her hands protectively around her head and waited for them to leave through the arched window openings. By the time Tom joined her, they had all gone – though the air was still full of the dust they had raised.

'Pfworr!' said Tom. 'It stinks up here.'

'Pigeons,' said Eva, screwing up her nose. 'I hate them.'

When Asa's head appeared at the hole, it was immediately clear there was something wrong. His face was as pale as wax. Eva and Tom ran to help him up onto the wooden platform.

'Are you all right?' said Tom.

Asa shook his head. 'Heights,' he said.

'Oh, Asa,' said Eva. 'You didn't have to come up.'

'I had the rope,' said Asa. 'And the torch.'

'But I could have carried them,' said Eva.

'I know,' said Asa. 'Thing was, by the time everything started spinning, it was already too late.'

150

Eva nodded sympathetically. 'You were very brave,' she said.

'I don't feel it,' said Asa. He looked down. 'This platform *will* hold, won't it?'

'It's been here for over a hundred years,' said Eva.

'That's what I mean!' said Asa, smiling weakly.

'Well,' said Tom, looking across at the bell, 'that's what we came to see.'

Eva smiled. 'It really is beautiful,' she said.

'For a million pounds, it should be!' said Tom.

He ran his fingers over the line of animals. *Marching two by two* was not enough to describe the intricate design of the pairs of animals – from elephants and hippos at the bottom, to squirrels and mice at the top – which wound their way round and round the bell. Eva crouched down and looked at the spiral of animals descending the inside: crocodiles chasing antelopes, following zebra, running after rhinos which, in turn, were loping after the elephants. A never-ending spiral; an endless cycle of life.

'How ironic,' said Eva, 'that something so, so beautiful could have led to so many ugly incidents.'

Tom and Asa said nothing. They were both thinking of one particular incident, the ugliest incident of all – the death of Jake Armitage.

'Right then,' said Tom at last, trying to sound optimistic. 'Let's shed a little light on the matter.' Asa handed him the torch.

They looked everywhere in the loft – in every nook and cranny, beneath and on top of the beams, even on the bell itself. But the hand was nowhere to be seen.

'Hmmm,' said Tom. 'I had the horrible feeling it wouldn't be up here. Silas Grimsby was on the scaffolding when his hand got stuck, wasn't he?' He moved to the edge of the hole in the floor and pointed. 'It must be down there, somewhere.'

'Tom,' said Eva. 'Are you sure you want to go down there?'

'I'm sure I *don't* want to go down there,' said Tom. 'But I haven't got much option, have I? You don't like pigeons and Asa doesn't like heights . . .' He grinned. 'I don't mind. Honest.'

'Well, at least tie the rope round you,' said Eva. Tom nodded.

He secured the rope tightly around his waist and looked for somewhere to attach it. The platform itself was no use because there was no way of getting to the beams, and the ladder was far too rickety to be trusted. In the end – although he didn't like the idea of entrusting his life to the bell – Tom knew he had no option.

With Asa's help, he climbed up on to the massive bell and tied the rope, several times, through the ring at the top. Satisfied that it would hold, Tom jumped back down on to the platform. He returned to the square hole.

'Here goes,' he said.

'Good luck,' said Eva and Asa together.

Below the platform, the air was immediately fresher. Tom felt his head clear. He knew what he had to do.

Rung by rung, Tom began to descend the first ladder. With every fourth step, he paused and shone the light round into the various cracks and crevices in the surrounding wall.

'Found anything?' Eva called down.

'Not yet,' said Tom, as he carefully manoeuvred himself round onto the third ladder.

As he spoke, he heard something above him: a creaking, grinding sound. It was the noise of the cogs and wheels lurching into action, preparing to chime the half hour. But Tom did not know this. To him, it sounded as though the whole platform was beginning to shift. Terrified, he wondered whether his weight was dislodging the bell.

Suddenly, the bell tolled. The sound of the clapper hammering against the inside of the brass bell echoed round the bell-tower like a bomb exploding. It was deafening.

Unprepared, Tom jerked with fear – and as he did so, his foot slipped from the rung. He tried desperately to cling on, but his fingers had seized up. As if in slow motion, he watched as they slid away from the juddering wood. The next instant, he was tumbling backwards through the air.

'AAAAAAARRGHH!' he screamed.

Falling. He was falling, away from the safety of the ladder and down towards the tiled floor which was racing up to meet him.

Suddenly, there was a sharp jolt. He had come to the end of the rope. The knot slipped, but held. The rope tightened round his waist. And there he hung – body outstretched, head down, and swaying to and fro like a pendulum. He was still clutching the torch.

'Tom!' Eva screamed. 'Are you all right?'

It took a moment for Tom to realize she was shouting at him. 'Yes,' he replied weakly. 'Only, get me out of here.'

Suspended there in mid-air, the floor below him looked so far away – and so hard. Thank heavens the rope held, he thought. Thank heavens I used it!

And then it occurred to him that what had just happened to him must also have happened to Jake Armitage. He, too, had lost his footing when the bell sounded. The difference being that Jake Armitage had not used a rope.

'An accident,' said Tom quietly to himself. 'That's what it was. A silly accident.'

Above him, he could hear the sound of Asa and Eva coming down towards him. He tried to turn round so that he could see them. This was a mistake. Not only was he unable to twist far enough around, but the movement made him slip. The rope slid down his waist until it was digging into his hips and – with the blood suddenly rushing to his head – his whole body began to turn.

And then Tom saw it!

In a small crevice in the wall, exactly level with his eyes, he caught a glimpse of something yellowy-white. Still turning, he lost sight of it before he could confirm what it was. As he came round again, however, he aimed the beam of the torch directly into the hole. This time there was no doubt. It was the hand. Not the ghostly manifestation with its sharp nails and ragged skin, but the bony remains of a real hand: the hand of Silas Grimsby.

'I've seen it!' he exclaimed. 'Eva. Asa. It's here!'

'Where?' said Eva excitedly, as she moved down onto the fourth ladder.

'There,' said Tom, pointing round behind him.

Eva peered into the darkness. 'Are you sure?' She turned back to Asa. 'Can you see anything?' she said.

Asa, by this time, was suffering from the whirling pits once more. His hands were wet, his mouth was dry; he couldn't swallow. 'N . . . n . . . no,' he stuttered.

Eva frowned. 'Look,' she said, 'I think you

ought to continue to the bottom.' She swung round to the back of the ladder and clung on tightly. 'Come past me,' she instructed.

Asa didn't need to be told twice. One by one, he continued down the rungs of the ladder, trying hard not to tread on Eva's fingers as he did so. When he was finally out of the way, Eva pulled herself back again and, as Tom spun round for a fourth time, she leant out, grabbed him by the arm, and pulled him towards the safety of the ladder.

'Thanks!' said Tom, as his feet finally came to rest on the rung. Never had something so flimsy felt so solid! 'It definitely *is* the hand,' he said, shining the light back into the hole. 'Look, there, you can see the thumb.'

Eva looked over the wall. She wasn't convinced – and, even if it was the hand, how were they going to get it? 'It must be three metres away,' she said. 'What . . .'

'I'm going to swing over,' said Tom. 'Like Tarzan,' he grinned. 'And don't say anything to try and put me off,' he added as Eva's face creased up with concern.

'But . . .'

'The rope's hanging in the middle,' he said, looking up. 'If you push me off, I can swing over, grab it and swing back. Piece of cake. The only thing is, you'll have to take the torch.'

Eva thought the idea ridiculous. It was *far* too

156

dangerous. On the other hand, she also knew that Tom was going to go ahead with the plan whether she liked it or not. When he gave her the word to push, Eva pushed.

Tom found himself flying across the void. As the wall got closer, he stretched out his arm. Unfortunately, the rope – which had wound itself round one way – now began to unwind itself. Tom's fingers scratched at the stonework, and came away empty handed.

'Push me again!' he cried out, as he swung back to the ladder. 'And keep the light steady.'

Eva did as she was told. Tom went swinging back towards the wall, faster than before. This time the rope did not turn. This time his outstretched hand headed straight for the hole. When he got close enough, he thrust his fingers into the crevice and closed them around the hard yellowy-white object.

'YES!' he cried.

As he swung back to the ladder with the hand in his grasp, Tom was surprised by how well he was reacting. He'd imagined that touching the hand would unleash a multitude of dark and irrational fears. But it hadn't happened. He wasn't even trembling. Though the spirit of the hand with its tattered frill of skin had been so terrifying, the actual skeleton was just that: a few old bones.

'Well done!' Eva exclaimed. 'Fantastic!'

'I know,' said Tom, grinning from ear to ear. 'We did it! You take the hand a sec – I'll go and untie the rope.'

Eva nodded and, as Tom climbed back up the ladder, she cradled the hand gently in both hands. 'Asa,' she called down. 'Tom's done it. We've got the hand.'

But Asa did not reply. He wasn't there. Unable to bear the sight of Tom swinging to and fro, he had gone outside. Though it was pouring with rain, getting wet was better than remaining in the chapel tower.

When the door opened behind him, he turned. Tom and Eva were standing there. From the look on their faces he knew that they had been successful.

'The hand!' he cried. 'Where is it?'

Tom held out his scarf and unwrapped it. There, lying in the soft brown wool – like a bony fledgling in its nest – was the hand.

Unlike biology lab skeletons, which are boiled till the bleached bones separate and then reconnected with wire, the hand was still intact, held together by the leathery tendons and ligaments. It was small – a child's hand – stiff and a curious shade of brown, like stained pine. Worst of all was the position of the fingers. They were splayed out and unbending, frozen in that final spasm of pain as the knife had cut through the wrist.

Tom realized there were tears welling up in his eyes. He sniffed. 'Come on,' he said, wrapping up the hand protectively, as if it would mind getting wet. 'Let's finish the job off.'

Together, he, Eva and Asa made their way round the chapel and up to the top end of the graveyard, where the body of Silas Grimsby – or, most thereof – was buried beneath the beech tree.

The rain, by now, was torrential. It lashed against their faces, driven on by the blustery wind. The skeletal trees bent and bowed, and far away in the distance the rumble of approaching thunder echoed along the horizon.

The three children stopped in front of the gravestone. Tom unwrapped the hand for a second time. 'You don't think we actually have to . . . to attach it.'

'What?' said Asa. 'You mean dig down two metres with our bare hands. You must be joking! No. *Here lieth the body of Silas Grimsby*,' he said, reading from the stone. 'As long as it's in his grave . . .'

He bent down, scraped away the slimy brown leaves, and began tearing at the wet grass underneath. 'Use this,' said Tom, handing him his knife. With the longest blade, Asa cut four deep lines in the grass and carefully levered out the square of sodden turf. Beneath the matted roots, the earth was dry and crumbly. It didn't take Asa long to dig down to the depth of his elbow. There he stopped. The thought of something grabbing him from below prevented him from going any deeper.

'That should do it,' he said. 'Pass the hand over.'

'No,' said Tom. 'I want to do it.' He knelt beside the grave, and slid the hand down into the hole. 'There,' he sighed, as the hand came to rest on the bottom. 'Back where you belong.'

Having filled in the hole again, Tom laid back the square piece of grass and patted it down. Then he stood up and took his place beside Eva and Asa. And as the three of them stared down at the small bump in the grave, tears mingled with the rain which streamed down their faces.

'I wish we'd thought of something to say,' said Tom at last.

'You mean like a prayer?' said Eva.

Tom nodded. Above him, the wind howled mournfully through the ancient beech tree.

'God bless,' said Eva softly.

'God bless,' said Asa and Tom.

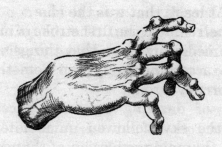

17

THE SECRET OF THE GRAVE

For the first time since he had arrived at Styles Grange, Tom felt at ease. It was as if, having been carrying a rucksack full of bricks, he'd suddenly been allowed to take it off.

Mr Baxter had finally been successful with the boiler and that afternoon he, Asa and Eva went swimming in the pool. Later, Miss Bennett gave her permission for them all to watch a film on television. And when lights-out came, they climbed into their beds happy – and not a little proud – that everything had turned out so well.

Tomorrow, they would go to see Professor Pritchard for a second time. They would tell him all about the hand of Silas Grimsby – and they would inform him of Miss Bennett's plans to sell the bell. At least, that was the idea.

As the bell chimed the first stroke of midnight, it was immediately clear that things were *not* going to go according to any plan. Something was wrong, horribly wrong.

A fork of dazzling lightning sliced down through the sky, followed immediately by a crashing, thumping explosion of thunder. Both Tom and Asa sat up at once. The lightning slashed again. And there, silhouetted against the window, was the hand.

The next instant, it erupted into a frenzy of rage. It flew at Asa and slapped him across the face, once, twice, three times, and cuffed him ferociously around the head. Then, without pausing, it darted over to Tom's cupboard, seized a pile of papers – their attempts to decode the passages in the diary – and flung them furiously into the air. The bell chimed again and the hand turned its attention to Tom himself. Leaping forwards, it smacked him across the ear.

'What?' he cried out, as the bell chimed a third time. The hand hit him again. 'What have we done wrong?' he bellowed.

Suddenly, the hand stopped. Then it leapt forward and grabbed him by the ear, the right ear – the same ear Miss Bennett had twisted so viciously. The bell rang a fourth time.

'No, NO!' Tom screamed. He was angry now. He'd risked his life to get to the hand, and this was the thanks he got. Reaching up, he tore furiously at the hand. 'Not like this!' he shouted. 'LET ME GO!'

The hand instantly released him. It flew off, stopped and half waved, as if in apology. The bell chimed five. Then, with finger crooked tentatively, the hand beckoned. Tom nodded.

He and Asa leapt off their beds and sped after the flying hand. The race was on.

As they passed the Baxters' room, they heard the sound of low murmuring. The couple must have been woken by the thunder. Up on their tiptoes, the pair of them crept along the corridor. Then, at the landing once again, they hurtled down the stairs, flight after flight.

This time the hand was not leading them to the library. Instead, it took them right down to the entrance hall, then back along the corridor, left, and out through the annexe door. The bell continued to chime. *Seven. Eight. Nine.* Again the question was whether they would reach the place the hand was leading them before the bell struck twelve.

Up past the annexe they ran, and on along the track. The clock chimed eleven.

'The bell tower!' Asa panted in alarm. 'It's taking us back to the bell tower.'

The hand stopped. It raised one finger: they should pay attention. Then it pointed. At that moment, the bell struck twelve. The hand

163

disappeared – but not before Tom had seen where it was directing them to go. Not the bell tower or the chapel itself – but to the graveyard.

As the storm continued all around them, Asa and Tom made their way to Silas Grimsby's grave. The lightning flashed and the thunder crashed, but the two boys saw and heard nothing. It was as though they were encased in a bubble that was keeping the world – the real world – at bay. Locked inside, they stumbled on towards the grave.

The moment they came up over the rise, they knew something was wrong. The ancient beech tree was tilting over at a precarious angle, threatening at any moment to complete its fall to the ground. As they got nearer, they saw that the roots of the tree had grown down, deep into Silas' grave. Now the tree had begun to topple, those same roots were opening the grave up.

All of a sudden a particularly powerful blast of wind tore across the graveyard. It was all Asa and Tom could do to prevent themselves being blown over into the hole. They staggered backwards, but remained standing. Not so the tree. With a pitiful creak, it gave in to the might of the wind and fell back. It landed with a crash, and was still.

Asa and Tom surveyed the damage. The gravestone had toppled over and was now lying on its side. The hand – rudely torn from its burial

164

place by one of the roots – was lying, fingers up, in a pile of dirt. Tom inched closer to the edge of the hole the uprooted tree had caused. He stared down.

'Look,' he said miserably.

Asa came closer and peered down into the darkness. 'What?' he said.

'Nothing,' said Tom. 'Absolutely nothing. The grave's empty!'

He crouched down and picked up the hand. As he did so, a trickle of earth ran down into the hole; the empty hole. Tom stood up and stared at the splayed fingers. He turned it over and sighed. 'What are we supposed to do with you?' he whispered. 'What?'

18

BREAKTHROUGH

The storm continued to rage as Tom and Asa made their way slowly back to their dormitory. They both felt distraught, despondent; it seemed as though the nightmare would never end.

It was only when they got back that they discovered they hadn't been the only ones to be disturbed by the thunder and lightning. Eva was sitting on Tom's bed next to Mister Bear, going through the pages of notes that the hand had tossed into the air. She looked up as they walked into the room.

'Where have you been?'

Tom waved his muddy foot at her. 'Guess,' he said.

'I . . .'

'To the grave,' said Asa. 'And do you know what? There's nothing in it. We buried the hand in an empty grave!'

Eva stared at him, mouth open. The body wasn't there. Suddenly, she realized that the discovery she had made with the diaries was important, after all. She turned to Tom.

'What does T17 mean?' she said.

'Transposition 17,' he explained. 'It means that A becomes the seventeenth letter of the alphabet.' He did a quick calculation in his head. 'P,' he said. 'No, Q. A becomes Q, B becomes R . . . Why?'

Eva smiled. 'Because I've found a message I understand,' she said. 'It's only short, so it might be a coincidence, but . . .'

'Where?' said Tom.

He and Asa raced over to the bed and looked down excitedly at the line Eva was pointing to. Just one of a series of apparently random succession of letters, it meant nothing to them. Asa shrugged. 'Son . . . dag . . . g-gsi . . .' he said, trying his best to pronounce the words. 'You understand *that*?' he said.

Eva nodded. '*So'n Dag gsi,*' she said, her voice suddenly deeper and more guttural. 'It's in dialect. Swiss German dialect.'

'Of course!' said Tom. 'Wolfgang Geisselhardt, he came from Zürich, didn't he?'

'So, what does it mean?' said Asa, still hardly

167

able to believe that the noise he had heard Eva making could actually mean anything.

'What a day!' said Eva.

'You can say that again,' said Asa. 'What with the tower, the hand, and now the empty grave . . .'

'No,' said Eva seriously. 'That's what it means. *So'n Dag gsi*. What a day! The diary entries are in English, but the coded passages are in German. Now all you've got to do is decode the rest of the passages,' she said. 'I'm sure they must be important.'

'We?' said Asa indignantly. 'What about you?'

'I?' said Eva. 'I shall translate. I don't mind swapping if you want?' she added. 'How *are* your Swiss dialects?'

Tom laughed.

'OK, OK,' said Asa. 'You win.'

Having drawn up two separate T17 conversion tables for themselves, Tom and Asa set to work on the passages. Tom took the first diary, Asa the second. Letter by letter, they transcribed the diary entries, passage after passage. And as they completed each one, they passed them to Eva, who wrote down her translation in an exercise book.

Hour after hour they worked. They couldn't stop now. They had to find out whether the diaries would reveal the final clue. If they did, the three children would be able to complete their task at last. If they did not, well, as

Wolfgang Geisselhardt himself had put it, 'Heaven help us all!'

As the time passed, so the storm receded. The rain stopped and the wind dropped, until the only noise in the dormitory was the soft scratching of pens on paper. Occasionally, Eva would gasp and read out a sentence or two she had translated out loud. Once, they were all surprised by the sound of an owl hooting from just outside their window. At half past two, the bell chimed.

Eva looked up. Her face was white. 'You can stop, now,' she said. 'I know enough.' She looked down at the pages of notes and cleared her throat. *'Things have gone from bad to worse . . .'* she began.

Asa and Tom listened in silence as Eva read out the decoded and translated passages from Geisselhardt's diary. It was soon clear that the truth of what had happened was far more bizarre than anything they could ever have dreamt up. Apparently, consumed with sudden guilt that he had cut off Silas' hand rather than risk damaging the bell, Wolfgang Geisselhardt had been unable to sleep. The boy's subsequent illness only made the situation worse. The unhygienic amputation had led to blood-poisoning, and the youth's condition quickly became critical. 'If he should die, then what will become of me?' Geisselhardt had written more than once.

And when Silas Grimsby *had* died, the entries again reflected the man's troubled state of mind. He agreed to Silas' last wish that he be buried in the chapel graveyard and saw to it, not only that the day he lost his hand be recorded alongside the date of his actual death, but also that the boy's dying words were carved onto a marble gravestone – 'the finest that money could buy'.

Then, three days after the burial of Silas Grimsby's body, something completely unexpected occurred. *Wie der Blitz aus heiterm Himmel,* as Geisselhardt put it. Like a bolt from the blue.

His housekeeper, Agnes, had returned sobbing from the chapel with the news that the grave – the grave of Silas Grimsby – had been robbed in the night.

Eva looked up. 'You see,' she said. 'The body's been missing for almost as long as the hand itself.'

'Then where is it?' said Tom.

'I'm coming to that bit,' said Eva. She found the relevant passage with her finger and began reading again.

I am beside myself with terror. Whatever malice the spirit of the boy might have harboured because of the missing hand will surely be multiplied a thousandfold now the body itself has been

170

snatched from its Christian burial place. I must retrieve the body!'

'And did he?' asked Asa excitedly. 'Did he get it back?'

Without looking up, Eva continued.

The destination of most of the stolen bodies, it turned out, was the medical university in town, she explained. There, a Dr Crisp would buy the corpses – no questions asked – for his students of surgery to practise upon. For a reason, unexplained in the diaries, Herr Geisselhardt and the doctor were acquainted.

The very last entry in the book recounted his intention to go to the university in search of the body.

'If the worst has come to the worst, and the corpse has already fallen under the surgeon's scalpels, then I might at least manage to save the skeleton. I hope Dr Crisp will have no objections to its being sent back to Styles Grange. Or rather, I pray not! And please God, when the body does return, might that then be an end of the matter. May Silas Grimsby finally rest in peace.'

Eva looked up. 'That's it,' she said.

'What? All of it?' said Asa.

Eva turned the page and showed them the note written there in pencil. *'Wolfgang Geisselhardt was thrown from his horse, returning from town. I do not know what he was doing there. He was killed instantly. Date of*

171

Death: 25.3.1869/Time of Death: app. 12 midnight.' It was initialled, E.P.

'Eric Pritchard,' said Tom. 'It's odd to think that the professor couldn't read Geisselhardt's last entry for himself.'

Asa shrugged. 'Fat lot of good it's done *us* being able to understand it,' he said. 'We'll never find out what happened to the body now.'

Eva looked impatiently from one boy to the other. 'I can't believe you two!' she suddenly shouted. 'I know it's late, I know you're tired – but WAKE UP! We're not talking about a body, we're talking about a skeleton. A SKELETON!' she said. She paused. 'You've already seen it!'

Tom felt icy panic shuddering down his back. He remembered the wardrobe door creaking open; he relived that awful moment when the skeleton inside had started to dance.

'STORM 9,' he heard Eva saying. 'The storeroom the hand tried so hard to lead us to. But it wasn't to find the hand – it was to find the rest of the body.'

'But . . . but why didn't they just bury it?' said Asa.

Eva shook her head. 'I doubt whether Geisselhardt confided in his staff. They wouldn't have known what to do with the skeleton when it suddenly arrived after his death.' She shrugged. 'I don't know. Perhaps it remained in a box; perhaps, when Styles Grange became a

172

school, it found its way into the biology laboratory. I don't know,' she said again. 'But one thing is certain, the skeleton up in Storeroom 9 belongs to Silas Grimsby.'

Tom frowned as he rummaged through the pockets of his trousers for the key. Surely he hadn't lost it. No. There it was, nestling at the bottom. He pulled it out and held it up in the air. 'Right then,' he announced, as he picked up the hand from the bed. 'Let's go and see.'

The Baxters were snoring loudly as the three children sneaked their way past their room once again. As Tom slipped the key into the lock of the storeroom door, the bell chimed five o'clock.

The three of them stepped into the room. Asa shone the torch at the far end of the room.

Because they were expecting it, the sight of the skeleton did not frighten them this time. At least, not so much. They walked closer. As they did so, Tom and Asa saw that the skeleton was smaller than either of them had remembered. The head, hanging from the rail, was on a level with their own – but the feet were suspended several centimetres above the bottom of the wardrobe. Closer still, and they all noticed something else – something that Eva, for one, could not believe. 'Two hands!' she exclaimed. 'But . . .'

They went right up to the skeleton and shone the torch inside the dusty wardrobe – first at the right hand, then at the left. Asa swallowed. 'Different,' he said.

Tom nodded, and made a closer inspection of the right wrist. The actual joint, he discovered, was made of plaster; it had been skilfully moulded to the end of the bone. To this, a hand had been attached. But not Silas Grimsby's hand: this hand was far too big for the rest of the body.

Asa carefully unscrewed the hand from the arm and laid it down on the floor. Then, without saying a word, he scraped away at the plaster to expose the splintered bone underneath. When he had finished, Tom took the smaller hand, the splayed hand – the hand of Silas Grimsby – and pushed it into place. The two halves of bone formed a perfect match. No trace of doubt remained: the hand and the body of that unfortunate youth had finally been reunited.

As he stared at the skeleton, Tom felt overwhelmed with sadness. He wasn't just looking at an anonymous collection of bones. This had once been a real person – a boy, only a couple of years older than himself. A boy with a name. Silas Grimsby. How unfair it was that he had fallen victim to the greed of the man he had seen as his benefactor. How cruel fate had been, first robbing him of his hand and then snatching him from his grave.

'We must bury it,' said Eva.

'Him,' Tom corrected her. 'We must bury him.'

At that moment, something happened. The wardrobe began, all at once, to glow with a cool blue light. Tom pulled back; he let go of the hand. Instead of dropping down to the floor, it remained where it was – at the end of the arm, where it belonged.

Unable to turn away, the three children continued to stare at the skeleton. As they did so, they became aware of a change taking place. The air immediately around the bones seemed to quiver and pulsate, like heat above a tar road in summer. Then – little by little and bit by bit – the quivering turned solid and the pulsations took shape.

Tom, Eva and Asa found themselves looking at a boy. He was thin but not skinny and his clothes, though patched, looked warm enough. While he was alive, Silas Grimsby had not been neglected. He was staring down at his hand. Slowly, tentatively, he wiggled his fingers around.

He looked up and his mouth and eyes smiled warmly. His lips parted. *Thank you*, they said.

Just then, the bell chimed the quarter hour. As the echoing sound faded away so, too, did the ghostly apparition of the smiling boy.

With the blue light gone and the skeleton back in place, Asa began to shuffle about awkwardly. 'Some kind of trick of the light,' he said.

'Or the lack of sleep,' said Eva uncertainly.

Tom smiled. 'The hand is still in place,' he said. 'And look!' he exclaimed.

The fingers had changed their position. Where, before, they had been rigid and splayed in that final agonizing spasm, now they were relaxed. The hand of Silas Grimsby was finally at peace. Soon, it would also be at rest.

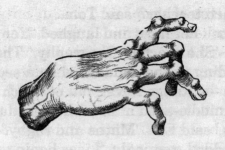

19

LOOSE ENDS

It was almost six when the children finally returned to the dormitory. Although they were shattered, sleep was out of the question. They were far too excited – and there was still so much to do.

It was Saturday. The new term started on the Monday. By then, it was important that everything had been sorted out. Together, the three of them sat down and made a short list of exactly what they had to do that day.

At seven o'clock, Tom heard a car coming up the driveway. He and Eva jumped up and looked out of the window as a young woman parked and climbed out of the car.

'It's Mademoiselle Leblanc,' she said.

'A French teacher?' said Tom.

Eva shook her head and laughed. 'Yes and no,' she said. 'She teaches Geography.' They were still standing at the window when a second car pulled up – a Range Rover, out of which jumped a stocky middle-aged man with short dark hair. 'Mr Miles,' said Eva. 'Maths and rugby.'

Tom nodded worriedly. 'I was hoping we'd get all this out of the way before everyone started arriving back,' he said.

Asa came over to join them. He pointed down at the car turning into the driveway. 'Mr Morris,' he said.

'Biology,' said Eva. She turned to Tom, and saw the troubled expression on his face. 'Don't worry,' she said.

Tom smiled, but remained concerned. It had been dangerous enough getting into the store-room before. With all these extra teachers around, it was bound to be even more difficult to return unseen. And if they were going to give a decent burial to the skeleton – whole once more – then one more visit to the room was essential.

'Come on,' said Asa. 'Let's get washed up and see if Mrs Baxter has got breakfast ready. I can't stand all this hanging around.'

Half an hour later, he, Eva and Tom were tucking into scrambled egg and sausages on toast. Half an hour after that, they were once again standing on the doorstep of Knapp

178

Cottage, waiting to complete the first task on their list of things to do: *Inform Professor Pritchard about Miss Bennett and the bell.*

The professor rubbed his hands together gleefully when he heard the news. 'I never liked that woman,' he said. His eyes narrowed. 'Just the type to vandalize a book,' he added. 'I can just see her snooping around in the library trying to find out how much the bell was worth, and then stumbling across details of the curse in my book . . .' He chuckled. 'Must have scared her half to death!'

Although it was many years since he had taught at Styles Grange, Professor Pritchard still knew several of the school governors. He promised not only to inform them about the suspected embezzlement of school funds, but also to alert the police to the imminent sale of the bell.

'The thing is,' he said, 'she'll probably deny everything. We need proof.'

'But we *heard* her!' Eva protested.

'Your word against hers,' said the professor shaking his head. 'No, what we need is concrete evidence to show that she's trying to sell the bell.'

'The letters!' Tom exclaimed. 'We sent off a whole load of letters to various antiques dealers.'

'Did you now?' said the professor excitedly. 'And when might that have been?'

'On Monday,' said Asa.

'Good,' said the professor. 'So they should have arrived by now. Can you remember any of the names and addresses? If we can give them to the police they'll be able to make inquiries.'

'Oh, crumbs,' said Tom. 'There was . . .' He struggled to picture the fronts of the envelopes. 'There was . . . *Archer Antiques*, though I don't know where it was. Oh, and . . . I remember!' he said excitedly. Suddenly, it was as if he was holding the letter in his hand. He only had to read the words. '*Grindlay and Swainson's Brass, Bronze and Copper Emporium*,' he said.

'Well done, my boy!' the professor exclaimed. 'That should be easy to trace.'

'Yeah,' said Asa. 'I've got one, too.' He put on his posh voice once again. '*Reginald Courteney Pringle, Esquire*. There can't be too many of them about!'

'Bravo!' cried the professor and clapped his hands together. 'Excellent work!'

Tom smiled to himself. The spirit of Silas Grimsby had only communicated with children – perhaps because he had been a child himself when he died; perhaps because he was unable to trust adults. Whatever the reason, whenever the hand had appeared, the children were on their own. Sometimes though, Tom now realized, it felt good to be able to let grown-ups take control of a situation.

180

It was as they were leaving that they discovered Professor Pritchard was also able to help them with number two on their list: *Find coffin.* If the skeleton was to be buried, they wanted to do it properly. Silas Grimsby deserved it.

That Christmas, Mrs Pritchard had received a full-length mirror, sent by her sister in Thailand. It had come in a long, thin wooden crate.

'Perfect,' said Tom, as the professor dragged it out of his shed. 'Are you sure we can have it?'

'My dear boy, it's the least I can do,' he said. 'Take it. Take it and go. I have several important telephone calls to make,' he said, his eyes twinkling. 'And then,' he added, 'I thought I'd do a spot of work.' He smiled. 'Thanks to you, *The Hauntings of Styles Grange* is going to need a final chapter!'

The three children were exhausted by the time they had lugged the box all the way back to the school. Not wanting to be caught, they turned left at the gates, cut through the woods and headed up to the chapel graveyard. There, they concealed it behind the fallen beech tree.

'Right!' said Tom, and wiped his brow. 'Time for number three on the list.'

By the time term started two days later on the Monday, several things had changed at Styles Grange. For a start, Miss Bennett was no longer to be seen – or heard – in her office. She had been suspended from her post and was awaiting trial for embezzlement. In her place, Mr Miles – the maths and rugby teacher – had been appointed acting head. The board at the end of the drive would have to be changed once again.

These, though, were superficial changes. More important, by far, was the change of atmosphere that had come over the school. Suddenly, instead of being cold and cavernous, it seemed light and airy, warm and cheery.

Some put this down to the absence of the icy Miss Bennett – and certainly, with the halls and corridors once again full of vases of flowers, it was more colourful. Tom, Eva and Asa knew, however, that the change in atmosphere at the school had little or nothing to do with change of principal. It had come about because Styles Grange itself had finally been released from the grip of the unhappy spirit which so often roamed its corridors. It had changed because Tom, Eva and Asa had done the right thing.

They'd had to. After all, it was on their list: *Bury Silas Grimsby*.

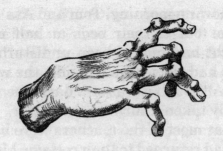

20

LAST WORDS

Although they would have liked to, it proved impossible to bury the skeleton that Saturday evening. There was too much coming and going around the school. Someone was bound to have asked them what they were up to. So it was that, at lights-out, the skeleton of Silas Grimsby – although complete once more – was still up in Storeroom 9.

'You don't think the hand will return again tonight, do you?' Asa had said, as he climbed into his bed.

'I hope not,' said Tom. 'No, I'm sure it won't. It's back where it belongs now. I don't think there'll be any more hauntings at Styles Grange.'

The following morning, Tom and Asa dragged themselves out of their beds at half past six. Their night had indeed been undisturbed, and both boys had slept well. Outside, the wind had dropped. Although it was still dark, the weather had clearly taken a turn for the better.

Now that most of the teachers were back, the Baxters had returned to their cottage. Mr Morris was in his room once more in the boys' half of the hallway, while Mademoiselle Leblanc was in her room in the girls' half. Both of them were notoriously light sleepers.

Asa and Tom held their breath as they tiptoed along the hallway. One creaking floorboard and they would surely be discovered. When they reached the girls' dorm, they found Eva already up and waiting for them. She had an empty backpack slung over her shoulder. The three of them greeted one another in silence, made their way cautiously down to the next floor and crept along to the row of storerooms.

'We'll find everything we need in here,' Tom whispered, as they reached the room full of theatrical costumes and props. They disappeared inside.

A few moments later, they re-emerged from the room. Tom was holding a spade, Asa was carrying a blanket, while Eva had a vase, two ropes and a candle in her backpack. They went to the next room. Storeroom 9.

With Eva in charge of the torch, Tom and Asa lay the blanket out on the floor, placed the skeleton carefully in the middle and wrapped it up.

'So far so good,' said Asa. 'Let's just hope we don't bump into anyone on our way out. I don't fancy trying to explain this little lot away.'

He needn't have worried. Nobody was up that early, and the three children managed to creep down the stairs, out through the annexe door and across the playing fields without being seen or heard.

It was just beginning to get light by the time they reached the graveyard and a wispy grey mist was coiling its way in and out of the headstones. An owl hooted from the branches of the fallen beech tree. As the children approached, it flapped its wings and glided off on padded wings.

Tom and Eva pulled out the box from behind the tree trunk and removed the lid. Tom lay the wrapped skeleton gently down inside it. Before they replaced the lid, he pulled the woollen cloth aside – just to reassure himself that the hand was there.

He smiled. Not only was it there, but it was still connected to the wrist as if it had never been severed all those years ago.

With Asa on one side and Eva and Tom on the other, they lowered the box down to the bottom of the hole, and dropped the ropes in on top. Then, taking it in turns, they all filled in the hole as best they could. This wasn't easy as much of the soil was caught up around the tree's exposed roots – but they managed it. And when Asa had replaced the headstone to its proper place, the grave was once again restored.

Eva pulled the vase from her bag and placed it in front of the gravestone. Tom filled it with sprigs of holly that he had sawn from the tree with the double-edged blade of his Swiss Army knife. Asa lit the candle and, having dripped some molten wax onto a stone, placed it next to the vase. Then the three children stood around the grave, hands clasped in front of them and heads bowed.

Before, when they had buried the hand, all of them had regretted that they had nothing to say to mark the importance of what they were doing. This time, each of them had come prepared. Tom cleared his throat.

> *'Here lies the body of Silas Grimsby,*
> *Whose searching can now cease.*
> *The hand is back where it belongs –*
> *May all now rest in peace.'*

Tom continued staring down at the gravestone when he had finished. It had taken him ages to think of a rhyme for 'peace'. Now he had said it, he felt self-conscious.

'Go on,' he muttered to Asa.

'All right,' Asa hissed back. He coughed and began.

> 'Here lies the body of Silas Grimsby,
> Who lost his hand when five and ten,
> But now, a hundred years later,
> He's got it back again.'

Tom and Eva had to stifle their laughter. They didn't want to hurt Asa's feelings. They didn't want to hurt *anyone's* feelings.

Eva took a deep breath, and looked back down at the grave. At that moment, the chapel bell rang out. It was seven o'clock. Like the atmosphere in the school, the sound of the bell had changed. Instead of the dark, ominous tolling that had echoed mournfully round the corridors of Styles Grange, its chimes now seemed brighter; in some way more full of hope. As it rang out, so Eva recited her verse.

It didn't scan, and the rhyme wasn't perfect, but Asa and Tom both thought that Silas Grimsby – if he could hear them – would appreciate Eva's parting words best of all.

'Here lies the body of Silas Grimsby,
Whose separated spirit roamed.
Finally, Silas Grimsby,
You are home.'

THE END

THE WAKENING
by Paul Stewart

*'One is dead, but not forgotten,
A name lived on when the body
was rotten . . .'*

Sam is scared – more scared than he's
ever been before. Each night, when he
goes to sleep, he dreams he is going to
the same place – a dark, silent forest,
choked with dense undergrowth.
And then the voices begin . . .

First he hears the children chanting – as if
they are playing some old game. Then, in
the centre of the forest, a hand claws its
way out of the ground. Someone – or
something – has been brought back to
life. What's more, it has come with an
astonishing message that Sam
cannot afford to ignore . . .

**'A tremendous pacy read with short,
punchy chapters'**
Books for Keeps

'Totally unputdownable'
The School Librarian

0 440 86347 3

CORGI YEARLING BOOKS

JACQUELINE HYDE
by Robert Swindells

I was bursting with energy, ready for anything. For the first time in my life, I was alive. Fully alive.

Jacqueline Hyde has always been a *good* girl. But from the moment she finds the little glass bottle in Grandma's attic, Jacqueline's life changes. Suddenly she's cheeky and loud, in with the roughest gang at school – Jacqueline *Bad*.

It's fun at first. Exciting. But then Jacqueline Bad gets into *serious* trouble. And although she keeps *trying* to be her old self, the bad side just won't let her go . . .

'Utterly believable . . . the breathless, short chapters make page-turning unavoidable'
Junior Bookshelf

0 440 863295

CORGI YEARLING BOOKS

CLOCKWORK
or ALL WOUND UP
by Philip Pullman

Tick, tock, tick, tock!
Some stories are like that. Once you've
wound them up,
nothing will stop them . . .

A tormented apprentice clock-maker – and a
deadly knight in armour. A mechanical
prince – and the sinister Dr Kalmenius,
who some say is the devil . . . Wind up these
characters, fit them into a story on a cold
winter's evening, with the snow swirling
down, and suddenly life and the story
begin to merge in a peculiarly macabre
– and unstoppable – way.

Almost like clockwork . . .

SILVER MEDAL WINNER,
1997 SMARTIES PRIZE
SHORTLISTED FOR THE WHITBREAD
CHILDREN'S BOOK AWARD
SHORTLISTED FOR THE
CARNEGIE MEDAL

0 440 863430

CORGI YEARLING BOOKS

THE GHOST DOG
by Pete Johnson

'I sensed hot breath on my neck. It was right behind me. It'll get me, I must run faster . . . faster . . .'

Only mad scientists in stories can create monsters, can't they? Not ten-year-old boys like Daniel. Well, not until the night of his spooky party when he and his friends make up a ghost story about a terrifying dog . . .

It's a story made up to frighten Aaron – tough, big-headed Aaron. But to Dan's horror, what begins as a ghost story turns into a nightmare. Each night the ghost dog – a bloodthirsty, howling monster – haunts his dreams, and Dan suspects that what he conjured up with his imagination has somehow become . . . real!

A spooky tale filled with chills and thrills, from top children's author Pete Johnson.

WINNER OF THE 1997 YOUNG
TELEGRAPH/FULLY BOOKED AWARD
WINNER OF THE STOCKTON-ON-TEES
CHILDREN'S BOOK AWARD

0 440 86341 4

CORGI YEARLING BOOKS